A Previous Life

Also by Margo Poirier and published by Ginninderra Press
Unzipped!
Et Cetera (Pocket Poets)
Wellspring (Picaro Poets)

Also by Margo Poirier and published by Mulberry Hill Publications
Moon Shards

Margo Poirier

A Previous Life

A Previous Life
ISBN 978 1 76041 474 0
Copyright © Margo Poirier 2017
Cover: Natasha E. Scholey

First published 2017 by
GINNINDERRA PRESS
PO Box 3461 Port Adelaide 5015
www.ginninderrapress.com.au

Margo Poirier

A Previous Life

A Previous Life
ISBN 978 1 76041 474 0
Copyright © Margo Poirier 2017
Cover: Natasha E. Scholey

First published 2017 by
GINNINDERRA PRESS
PO Box 3461 Port Adelaide 5015
www.ginninderrapress.com.au

Prologue

Seventy witch trials took place from the mid eighteenth century to the early twentieth century, as well as numerous prosecutions involving cunning folk. The majority of these date from the nineteenth rather than the eighteenth century partly because there was greater concern over the continued belief in witchcraft then and also because the introduction of a professional police force facilitated the lodging of official complaints.

James Augustus St John wrote,

> here in England in the midst of our civilization, with the light of Christianity ready to pour into the meanest and darkest hovels [violence against witches was] still prevailing in our rural districts while the belief in witches is all but universal.

There were numerous women with the scars to prove it. In 1935, a doctor from Poole, Dorset, wrote about an old woman of his acquaintance whose back and chest were covered with scars from being scratched.

1

Dick lay with his ankles crossed, his hands clasped behind his head and his mouth set in what had recently become a habit. He was aware he had dug his heels in, to use a clichéd expression, and that Chloe was becoming irritated by his taciturn behaviour. But he couldn't explain it, at least not to her, because she was a part and, if he was honest, a good part. Probably, if he was really, really honest, the major reason. She had harped on and on about his decision to take early retirement. Truth was, he had wanted to take earlier retirement! He wasn't married to the law so it was easier, but the ice in the atmosphere was palpable.

'Well, it's all very well for you,' she'd said. 'I still have commitments to my clients and wouldn't let them down. It's not all fun for me, you know, and if you retire, we'll be dependent on the one income.'

Chloe didn't mention that her salary more than matched his and they would do well enough. The house was paid off, there were no dependants (another sore spot not up for discussion any more as the clock now said no).

Dick sighed. He glanced over to his wife's side of the bed. She would be coming through the front door by ten. On the dot. Not a stroke before or after. She was punctual, reliable, maintained a tidy house, cooked, if not well, adequately. She attended the Universal Christian Women's local chapter meeting on the first Wednesday of every month. Lately there had been extra meetings and thereby could be the rub. She had never missed one of these meetings, not since she had found God. Dick had once joked about where she might have found him – under the bed, on the roof, in the freezer at the supermarket – but was met with a look that could kill at twenty paces. He hadn't tried it since. She kept herself very fit, an asset in the bedroom in the early days. He smiled wryly.

He was glad he wasn't a woman so he couldn't be persuaded to join the Universal Christian Women's movement. He had nothing against women, liked being up against them physicall,y and he sniggered a little; but as for being in the presence of droves of them all talking at once, surging forward as one mass of seething feminine energy, well, he found it disconcerting. And he was talking with some experience. Early in their marriage, he had been coerced into going with Chloe to a rally, only to discover that it was a huge get-together of some five hundred women who were protesting against unfairness in the workplace. Not a car in sight. To pull out at the last minute would have been bad form, so he stuck it out. Having come off very much the worse for wear with sunburn, a shirt in tatters from being grabbed by an over-zealous protester with huge knockers, and a shattered ego from listening to tirades of women complaining about their male employers, Dick vowed to enquire carefully about any invitation issued in the future.

Dick's mouth tightened even more when he thought about his present dilemma. He had enjoyed being married when Chloe was a sweet, gentle woman, but now – now she appeared distant, almost disconnected from him.

'Chloe love, pass the paper, would you? Chloe?'

She didn't seem to hear and finally when she turned towards his request, she seemed to be off elsewhere.

'Are you OK?' he would often ask her.

'I'm fine. Why do you ask?' a note of irritation in her voice.

'Well, it's just that… Oh, for Christ's sake! What planet are you on? I'm trying to make this work but you! You are just not responding! What's the matter with you? Ever since you joined this bloody bullshit cult, I just can't reach you any more. Why don't you just move in with one of your creepy friends? You care more about them than you do about me. If that's what makes you happy, just do it!' He'd gone too far but it was too late to take it back.

'Look, Chloe,' he softened a little. 'I'm sorry if I sounded a bit over the top, but really, you need to take a good look at what you're doing. And where it leaves us. Don't you care?' His words hung in the air like the smell of cooked cabbage.

'Umm,' Chloe would answer absent-mindedly. It was as if she didn't hear a word he had said. He felt dismissed. Again. It was like living with a stranger and even when she was in the room, she'd hide behind her long, corn-coloured hair, head bent over some task or other. He had mentioned a while back that he really hated being called Richard and could she call him Dick.

'What's wrong with Richard? It's very noble. It's a strong name. I don't know why you don't like it.'

'It's so formal. And I've been telling you for years that I don't like it but you insist on calling me a name I don't like! It's my name and I decide what I shall be called! You're starting to sound like my mother! Why don't you take any notice? It's…it's hurtful.'

'I think you have major problems about ageing.' She prodded. 'You have your hair cut like a teenager. You think that Dick sounds younger than Richard. Isn't that it?'

'No,' he protested vehemently. 'It's just a personal choice I would very much like you to respect.'

Was an argument about a name reason enough for leaving her? He didn't smoke, so couldn't wander off to the corner shop on the pretext of buying a packet of cigarettes and then disappear; forever maybe, to parts unknown. He had the will but not the imagination to concoct a believable disappearing plan. He had heard of people who left their car in an airport car park, taken a plane to Bolivia or some unlikely place and were never seen again. Were there cannibals in Bolivia, he wondered?

He checked the time. His heart was beating a little faster and seemed to be louder than usual. Chloe would be pulling into the driveway at precisely one minute to ten. He had one hour minus a minute to make a decision.

2

Dick reached into his pocket for some change to buy a ticket and drew out some very strange money indeed. Where was the five dollars he remembered being there? The two coins were unfamiliar but on further examination appeared to be old English florins. His hand pulled out a train ticket of some sort. Upon it, in crude writing, was London Town. Looking up and down the platform, he was intrigued by the clothes the commuters were wearing. There must be a fancy dress convention or something happening and they were all going by train.

The train whistle blew loudly and clouds of steam hissed and billowed up into the crisp morning air. Diesel train must be in for repairs. Dick shivered, noticing that the toes he began to tap to keep warm were encased in shoes with large buckles. His trousers were tapered in to just below the knee and he was wearing thick white stockings. Oh, for shite's sake! This just wasn't happening. He was aware of a slight shadow over his face and putting his hand up felt the shape of a hat with an upturned brim. By Jove, he heard himself muttering, realising at the same time that he had never before used the expression. He looked about and noticed that all the men and the young boys were dressed in similar attire.

Another blast from the train's whistle brought people dashing towards the carriage doors. Not wanting to be left behind to wonder about his fate, Dick ran and just made it, jumping into the last carriage. Slamming the door behind him, he began to walk down the narrow corridor, off which were small compartments. Most of them were fully occupied, the occupants chattering happily, unpacking large wicker hampers of food which they passed around to their companions.

'Pork pie, luvvy?' A hand reached out to him. 'Come in here with us. Look as if you've missed breakfast, you do. Wake up late, did we?'

A titter of laughter rippled through the compartment. It was all in good humour but Dick felt a flush of embarrassment creep over his face. He accepted the tasty-looking pie.

'I've not been in bed, actually. Awake all night, thinking. But I did miss breakfast. In a hurry to leave. I found myself on the station and here's the thing: I don't remember getting there – nor do I remember dressing in these…' he pointed to his stockings. 'Are you all going to a fancy dress convention or something?'

More tittering. A man in the corner seat near the window made a sign with his finger pointing to his head.

'What's a fancy dress convention?' the pork pie woman asked, brushing some errant crumbs from her comfortable chin.

'Well, you're all dressed in period costume,' replied Dick, feeling a little foolish by now.

'Luvvy, now you listen to me,' said Mrs Pork Pie. 'We is dressed as we always dress and there's no one who says different! If you ask me, you're the funny one in this carriage, appearing out of nowhere with your strange questions. Had a bit of the old snifter last evening, did we? Can't remember if you're comin' or goin'? Well, you're goin' as we're goin'. This train's taking us to London Town.' She sat back, chose a large piece of seed cake from the basket and began to munch as she looked out of the window.

Her fellow travellers took her lead and ignored Dick as they resumed chatting amongst themselves.

Dick's head was throbbing with confusion, anxiety and a distinct sense of disorientation. He leaned back against the seat, closed his eyes and tried to think. It had to be a dream, but if he was dreaming it, how come he was able to think that he was in a dream?

He'd had plans to escape an unhappy marriage, but he would have preferred going to a forward-thinking city in Europe where he could blend in with the crowd and restart his life. But this?

The rhythmic bumping of the train wheels on the track eventually sent Dick into a deep sleep. He dreamed that he was about to board the tunnel train to Calais. He dreamed of fresh goat's cheese, a little *vin du pays*, a nice *auberge* where he could spend a couple of days while he planned the rest of his life. The background music of the thumping train wheels and hissing of the steam as it hit the cold winter air pushed his dreams along.

'Hey, mister! Mister! Wake up! Stop yer snoring now. It's time to change trains. Come on now, wakey-wakey!' Mrs Pork Pie was shaking him by the shoulder and Dick started, jumping up in fright.

The occupants of his compartment, complete with baskets, surged through the narrow door and Dick was carried out on this human wave towards the station. He looked about him. There was no hint of what station this might be. He felt as if he was travelling with the folk of the faraway tree to one of the lands at the top of the magic tree. He decided he would have to be a part of his dream as there seemed no alternative. Once he had made the decision, he felt remarkably calm.

'Does another train come by, or do we have to go to another station,' he asked politely of a tall, thin young man standing beside him whistling under his breath.

'No. This be the only station. They takes this train here to the yard and brings another and we get on that one.'

'But why bother to change the trains at all? Seems a waste of time to me.'

'You're not from these parts, are you? Engine needs a rest. We gets a new driver and all and two extra carriages and we be off to London town.' He smiled down at Dick. 'See?'

'Not really, but I'll take your word for it. I have to ask, why two extra carriages?'

'Well, for the pigs and goats, that's why.' The young man shook his head and moved away to avoid further questioning.

After about an hour, Dick guessed – his watch had mysteriously gone walkabout and was not on his wrist – a handful of pigs and goats appeared at the end of the station and he watched as they were shepherded towards a ramp and led onto the train by an old farmer dressed in a battered smock and leather leggings. The farmer didn't reappear and presumably was going to stay with his animals for the journey.

Another hour or so passed and Dick was getting edgy. He was anxious to get to the bottom of his mystery but had no option now but to board the train as it was now coupled and hissing its impatience to get moving. To his amazement, his former companions were determined he should rejoin them and so he too was shepherded into another carriage where, in due course, more food appeared from their seemingly bottomless hampers. As Dick had brought nothing with him to eat, he was only too grateful to be included in this motley family of travellers.

Dick's snores blended with the other snoring sounds in the carriage as the train bumped its way towards London Town. After some hours, he awoke suddenly by a sudden movement of the train. Much shouting could be heard. The women in his compartment drew their children to them. Dick sensed fear in the air and abruptly stood up to look out of the window. The train had indeed stopped, but it was not in London, he was sure of that. A mixture of steam and fog made it difficult to see clearly, but he was sure he saw some horsemen down the track a little. More shouting, then sounds of screams as running feet approached his compartment. The door was thrust open and a masked man in black riding breeches and a three-cornered hat waved a very ancient pistol at them and demanded money and jewels.

Dick was so flabbergasted – yes, that was the word all right. A highwayman? On a train? Surely they only robbed horse-drawn carriages. But he reminded himself that he was in a dream where anything could happen and it apparently was happening. One minute he had been lying on his wife's cream and beige duvet and the next he was being held up by highwaymen on a steam train bound for London Town in what must be the year of 1779 or thereabouts. He smirked to himself.

'Hey, you! Ye think this is funny, do ye? Well, you'll not be laughing when you're strung up in yonder tree.' The highwayman pointed with his pistol. 'Now, hand over yer money and that ring on yer finger.'

'You can't have that. It's all I have and I don't have any money either.'

'A well dressed man about town like yourself and no money? A likely story.' The pistol moved closer to Dick's face. 'Now hand it over.'

Dick decided to comply, if not for his own safety but for the safety of his companions who were clearly poor but good folk. Even so, following his example, they threw down onto the carriage floor what precious things they did have. The highwayman scooped them up, greedily stuffing them into a pouch hanging from his waist. For good measure, he fired a shot into the ceiling of the compartment. Dick had never owned any gunpowder but he knew enough about it and had once seen a demonstration using it. The acrid smoke from the gunpowder clouded the air, aggravating everyone's nostrils. The women screamed; the children began to cry and the robber laughed like a character from an old movie and backed out with his loot. They heard running footsteps, a slamming of carriage doors and as Dick dared to look out of the window again, he saw six highwaymen mount their steeds and gallop off into the foggy distance.

It was some minutes before the train began to move and as the steam increased with pressure in the engine, eventually gathered speed and the little company of travellers sighed with relief as they comforted their children.

'Here, luvvy.' Mrs Pork Pie handed Dick a generous portion of bread with a lump of questionable roast meat hanging precariously from it. 'We is all a bit shaken from this terrible experience. Eat. Get your strength back. How brave you was to talk back to that nasty robber.' She smiled at him in admiration.

'Thank you,' said Dick rather meekly, not feeling brave at all but more at a loss than ever at his predicament. 'Does that sort of thing happen much?'

'Oh, all the time, dearie. All the time. You'd think we'd get used to it but, no, it's still a shocking experience. But they didn't get it all. Oh, no. Lookee here.' She hoisted one of her many skirts to reveal a large cotton bag attached to the inside of her petticoat. 'This is where I keeps me valuables. Them crafty buggers don't know nuffink. Sorry about your wedding ring, dearie.' She seemed genuinely concerned.

'Oh, that.' Dick wasn't about to explain that it had lost its significance a long time ago. 'Don't mention it.'

'Wouldn't do for a woman to wear a ring,' she continued. 'Far too dangerous. When they be difficult to take off, the highwayman is just as likely to cut off the finger. Terrible! Terrible tales I've heard, I have!'

Dick wondered if his finger would have been cut off had the ring proved difficult to remove. He shuddered.

'Anyway, I'm sure your missus will understand particularly when you tell her what happened, and you can buy her another when we reach London Town. Mind you, you will have to be careful – there are some shifty characters who'll sell you rubbish, mark my words.'

Dick promised he would mark her words and slumped down into his seat, full of bread and roasted meat. He slept. Highwaymen and black as soot horses galloped through his dreams and stayed until another jolting hailed their arrival in London Town.

Dick was beginning to realise that his dream was becoming a very nasty reality. He had no money, no job, no references, no contacts and soon there would be a parting of the ways with his carriage companions. He was in serious, serious trouble. He was beginning to envy his previous life. Or was this his previous life?

London Town station was big. Throngs of people and animals crowded the platform.

'Bye, luvvy,' called out Mrs Pork Pie as she shepherded her brood from the train and down the platform. 'Watch out for them scallywags, now.' She waved cheerily and her little family was soon swallowed up in the business of platform traffic.

Dick stood, feeling like a bewildered orphan. He was not part of this world but knew if he was to survive he must make a move. One step, then another out of the station and into the streets.

Moving like a blind man, Dick eventually found himself out in the street confronted by a very unfamiliar London.

3

Dick looked over his shoulder at the station behind him. He froze. The station had completely and utterly disappeared. Vanished as if it had never existed. Feeling hot and cold panic running up and down his entire body, Dick began to tremble with fear. He turned around again half expecting to see the train he had just left only minutes before, and that his disorientation had played a trick on him.

But there was no train, no station, no passengers that he recognised either. No evidence that his journey had ever taken place. His equilibrium now returning, Dick tried to make some sense of his predicament. Of course the train and disappeared along with the station. It had never existed! Trains had not yet been invented and he was clearly in a time long before that.

He began walking, stumbling now and again on the rough cobblestones. No one stared at him, no one took the slightest bit of notice that a man from another century was in their midst. But he looked just like any other citizen, dressed as he was. His fear subsided a little as the stark reality slid into his being. This wasn't a dream. This was another time and he had somehow stumbled into it and now he was trapped. Dick kept on walking, hoping some solution would miraculously appear. If the matter wasn't so serious, he could almost have laughed.

'Right, Sherlock, me old mate,' he muttered to himself, 'just keep moving until you can find a possibility.'

The stench of a city without sanitation assailed his nostrils, along with other smells of wet horses and the raw sewage he saw running down the streets in the open drains. Gagging, he began to run in the hope of finding a street that didn't stink like a compost heap but it was all the same. The buildings were built in a very haphazard fashion,

leaving a jumble of narrow, unlit passageways between residences and shops. He could well imagine that at night, these narrow lanes would be very dicey indeed. He saw no semblance of order anywhere.

Under a darkening sky, Dick shivered, partly from the cold and partly from uneasiness. He pulled up his collar tight about his neck. Without warning, a deluge struck and the rain pummelled him and penetrated his flimsy coat – no match for such weather. He tripped over something in the blinding rain and looked down to see a large rotting rat lying in an open drain that was now carrying sludgy water, refuse, excrement and God knows what else. Horse-drawn carriages with their heavy metal wheels splashed through large puddles and Dick copped his fair share of the putrid muck that abounded in the streets.

Things couldn't get much worse but he had to push on. Perhaps if he could find a dry spot for the night, by morning he would see clearly what sort of prospects he might have. How on earth would he find some work to earn a little money? He was not a prosperous lawyer here. He might as well be on Mars. It was frighteningly apparent that he was irretrievably lost between two worlds and could easily finish up lying in one of the dreadful drains.

With such dark thoughts on his mind, he crashed headlong into a man who, also with head bowed against the driving rain, hadn't seen him. They both reeled back. To Dick's astonishment, the man apologised and doffed his high hat, bowing slightly and muttering something inaudible. As the only person Dick had encountered so far who appeared civilised, he took a chance and replied.

'No, it was my fault, I'm sure. I'm very new to London Town and don't know my way about yet.'

'Quick! In here.' The man gestured towards a shop entrance. 'Bit dryer in here. So you're new to London Town? I must say I'm a little intrigued by your very strange way of speaking and I hope you don't mind me mentioning it.' Greying whiskers covered a good part of his face; pince nez glasses balanced on the end if his longish, tapered nose and he looked very much like a drenched blackbird.

'Not at all. I don't mind. You're the first person I've spoken to since my arrival this morning.'

'And from where did you come, pray?'

'Well, the thing is, I'm not sure. Not sure at all. At first I thought I might be having a dream but now, I'm sure I'm not. I wanted to escape and found myself travelling to London.'

'Escape? From what? Are you a criminal? I'm a magistrate myself and have some experience in these matters. Perhaps I could help you.' He looked intently at Dick.

'Criminal? Good lord, no! I'm actually a lawyer. That is, I was until…well, until all this happened.'

'A lawyer! Do you work for the law somewhere?'

'Well, back in 1997 I do!' Dick saw the funny side of his conversation with the magistrate, who clearly was not on the same page.

'You mean 1797, surely.'

'No. I fell asleep in 1997 and now I'm here. I'm cold, wet, without a job, without clothes and getting right pissed off. I might ask you if you have any idea where I could sleep the night and whether you might know of anyone who could give me a job.' Dick paused for breath, fearing he had gone too far, been too rude to this gentleman, for that surely was what he appeared to be.

'My good man, yes, I can see your predicament. It has affected your thinking somewhat but I do believe I can help you. If you will follow me, I can at least see that you get something to eat. That's a good start, is it not? Come.' And without further comment, he stepped out into the rain.

Dick followed. Within ten minutes or so, the gentleman stopped before a high, black iron paling fence. He pushed at the gate indicating for Dick to follow him up three large, stone steps. He inserted a key into the keyhole of a heavy oak door which swung into the hallway of a house shrouded in darkness. Dick discerned a faint glow that came closer and belonged to a squat little woman who held a candle in one hand and a taper in the other.

'Evenin', sir.' She dipped to a curtsy and proceeded to reach up to a bracket on the wall which held a gas lamp.

As the hallway became flooded with gaslight, Dick at last saw clearly the man who had come to his rescue. 'I can't begin to thank you,' he stammered, offering his hand.

'Not at all. Mellie here will find us some bread and cheese and I'm sure I have a small drop of port which will warm your victuals. And mine,' he added with a slight chuckle. 'And then we will talk a bit. By the way, my name is Henry Fielding and I live here with my brother John, who is also a magistrate but has a title and is called "Sir".' He gave a little laugh, obviously finding this amusing. 'He writes music too but I don't understand any of it. I dabble a little with the written word.' He chuckled again. 'I think you and I might be in the same business and perhaps we can help one another.'

Dick followed him into a large front room dominated by an imposing fireplace in which burned a coal fire. On an oval table, beside a black leather stitched chair with huge wings, sat a decanter in which glowed the viscous rubyness of port.

'Do sit, er...'

'Dick. The name's Dick.' Dick sat.

'Not Dick Whittington, I hope,' chortled Henry, pleased with his joke.

'No, just plain Dick. Dick Fortescue. I've never ridden a horse. At least, I don't think having a few riding lessons as a small child counts for much, do you?'

'Well, I suspect it doesn't matter now. I'm sure it would come back to you if necessary. You're here and must carry on with your life as it finds you.' He passed a full glass of the ruby port to Dick.

'Wisely spoken, but just how I'm not sure.'

'Let's drink to good luck then, shall we? Now, before you close your eyes, let me say that I have been looking for someone to help me with my work. As you may or may not know, John and I share a few rather modern ideas of how to impose some sort of justice on this society you see out there.' He waved a hand in the direction of the street. 'We hope to be able to reform young offenders and, er, women of the street as well. We are starting a system of record-keeping to share with other magistrates and the workload is proving bigger than we had at first thought. I am asking you, with your knowledge of the law, if you would be so kind as to help us. Will you? Of course, you would be paid a meagre wage at first, but later…'

'I don't know what to say, er, Henry, if I may call you that. I'd be delighted to help. Have you got an efficient police force in London Town?'

'Well, I'm afraid they do nothing much more than escort prisoners to the gallows or, at best, collect county taxes. And many of them are more corrupt than the criminals they should be chasing! But we have to start somewhere and another pair of hands would be welcome.'

Dick took a quick swallow of the port. 'I would like to help but I'm feeling very sleepy right now. Could we discuss this further in the morning, do you think?' Dick yawned uncontrollably.

Henry nodded. 'Of course. Come with me. There is a small box room adjoining the kitchen. It will be warmer in there and after a good night's rest, we will talk further.'

Dick sank gratefully on to his bed. His previous life seemed as far away as the moon and probably was. He slept soundly without dreaming.

The following morning, he instinctively reached for his wife beside him until he remembered. He blinked in the weak sunshine filtering in through a window high above him. No cream and beige duvet brushed his growing beard; no smell of freshly brewing coffee titillated his nostrils; no sound of Andy the dog barking at the chooks. The hessian bags on his mattress had made his skin itch, but he had prospects at last. He would soon be employed, could soon buy some clothes and could help as a vanguard in establishing the law of the land in which he lived. As he began to drift off, he wondered why Henry hadn't quizzed him further about his circumstances. It almost didn't seem to matter to him.

4

'Is the man deaf?' Chloe muttered under her breath, sighing and opening a fresh packet of analgesic mini tabs. She swallowed two with a large glass of water. Her headache was coming back. Really, if she wasn't able to get out of the house one or two evenings a week to go to her meetings, she'd be in a mental facility by now. It was one of the few things that kept her on track. That and her running. She had always run just because she loved it. She had run since she was about six years old and in adulthood had kept it up, competing in athletic competitions and winning some trophies.

She wasn't ambitious to plunge into an Olympic arena, and she never examined why she ran. Her father sometimes called her Fleetfoot. He had been proud of her. Richard didn't seem to care that she kept in shape. He wasn't like her father at all. When she ran, she was like a free spirit, soaring above herself into a place where her troubles couldn't follow. Was she running towards something or running away from something? It kept her very fit. Her clients often would comment about how healthy and young she looked and what was her secret? She would smile demurely and brush off the compliment. But secretly, of course, she was pleased, and her reflection in the bedroom mirror confirmed the comments.

Now it irked her to have missed her routine morning walk. She needed it like a drug. But she couldn't go now; not until she had found what had happened to Richard. Her head thumped and she lowered herself gently onto the living room couch to wait for the painkillers to kick in, massaging her temples gently with her fingertips.

Richard and his monologues appeared on the inside of her eyelids. She had come to see them as boring. Surely he hadn't always been like this? What had happened to the charming, flirty man she had married nearly twenty-five years ago? Perhaps he was on the edge of a midlife crisis. And he was becoming very untidy. He never took out the garbage, hardly ever helped with the washing up, was monosyllabic when she tried to engage him in conversation and was altogether becoming very disagreeable.

'Couldn't you just look for another position with someone else? Wouldn't that be enough of a change? You don't have to retire. That's just silly. Any firm would be glad to have you, I would have thought. You're a good lawyer. Why don't you just think about it for a bit?' Chloe felt a frown appearing on her forehead.

'I'm sorry, Chloe. But I've made up my mind.' He turned his attention to the chops and mashed potatoes in front of him.

'I see,' she replied tightly, seeing that his mind was indeed made up. Then she tried something else. 'Richard, do you think we could slip away for a bit of a break somewhere? You know, after you retire, if you like?'

'A bit of a break? Whatever do you mean? You're the one who never has enough time. Face it, Chloe, we've had plenty of opportunities to do just that. But with your precious meetings that have taken over your life not to mention your interior decorating work...'

'No need to be so sarcastic, Richard,' she interrupted. 'I just thought, that's all, with your being so non-communicative lately, that a change would do you – well, us – the world of good.'

'Non-communicative? Me? It's you who's never home to communicate. And when you do, it's always about the group. I don't give a shit about your group. Why would I be interested in anything they do, an idiotic bunch of bored women? I don't know how you stand it. Well, if I want to talk, I want to discuss something more relevant to life!'

'I see,' Chloe replied quietly. 'So you're not interested in anything I do, are you? It always has to be about you, doesn't it? Honestly, I don't know why I bother trying to help.'

'Did I ask you for your help? Did I?' Dick needled. 'Just leave me alone. Why don't you go for another run and give us both a break,' he added a little acidly.

So Chloe did. And for one whole week, she didn't say anything at all to him unless it was absolutely necessary. If she had to, she could very well manage by herself. It occurred to her that their marriage might well be at the end of its life. She often wondered how and why couples stayed married anyway for fifty years or more. It seemed extreme. Their twenty-fifth wedding anniversary was looming next month. Dick probably wouldn't remember and if he did it would be at the last minute. It had been a very long time indeed since they had been out to dinner to celebrate.

Chloe was becoming more and more convinced as she waded through the negatives that there was very little left of their relationship. Yet she couldn't bring herself to raise that topic just now. There had been good times, hadn't there? She searched her memory to recall a recent one and came up with a blank. She even wondered if he was seeing someone but couldn't bear to know and began attending more meetings during the week, sometimes at different venues. Occasionally, she would meet some friends and have dinner with them rather than go home to a sullen partner who didn't seem to care if she was there or not. And she ran.

Chloe reflected on her last conversation with Dick. A deep sigh heralded the beginning of tears but Chloe fought them back. She never saw her mother cry, even though she had had good reason. Although Chloe was only six years old, the memory of her mother's grieving for a dead daughter remained etched in her mind. Back then, what did a girl of six know about life and its misfortunes? She had felt sad at losing her twin sister too, without totally understanding and with no explanations given.

Looking later at the few photographs she had, she could see the uncanny likeness and it always brought a pang of grief for that other half of her taken so early in life. How her mother must have suffered living with an alcoholic husband trying to deal with grief in his own way. And yet Chloe's dad was not a violent drunk and he never hit her or her mother. That was something at least. Money was always short, as most of it went on drink. Chloe had been determined to marry a man who didn't drink and had a good job, with prospects. And Dick did. He didn't drink. Well, not back then he didn't. She had noticed lately that a few empty beer bottles had found their way into the garbage bin but when she confronted him, he accused her of being unreasonable. She had become angry and shouted at him. She was not going to put up with a drinker the way her mother had done. He looked hurt and she expected him to shout back but he didn't. He just shut down. What was wrong with the man?

Now their only communication took the form of an argument.

'Dick?' she called out again.

'Dick? Are you up there? Dick, I'm home. Do come down and put the kettle on. I'm dying for a cup of tea.' She tried to inject a little more caring into her voice, feeling just a little bit guilty that she may have misjudged him. 'Oh, it was a lovely evening, darling. I shall tell you all about it over tea.'

But darling didn't answer. Darling didn't answer because he didn't hear. Darling's still warm body imprint remained on his side of the pristine beige and cream duvet, but darling was not there.

5

'My dear, whatever do you mean?' one of her socialite friends had commented when she had aired this concern at a coffee morning. 'What is NQR when it's at home?'

Chloe sometimes wondered if some of her rather denser women friends were 'not quite right' as well and she had just shrugged and changed the subject. She wondered about many things, including her marriage and her desperate attempts to put some distance between her and Richard without ever actually physically leaving him. That would have meant that she had failed and Chloe hated failure of any kind and perceived it as a weakness. She disliked failure in others too but that was beyond her control. Her head continued to thump.

'Shut up!' Chloe yelled at Andy. 'I'm sick of your barking. Why didn't you leave too?'

Richard was not in the bedroom. He was always here, always waiting for her to come home, predictable with his waiting to the point where she wished he'd do something drastic for a change and leave a note to say that he was drinking at the pub and wouldn't be home until all hours. Yet strangely she was put out by his absence. Now the only drastic thing he was about to do was to retire.

Drifting in and out of a restless sleep that night, Chloe kept looking at the little bedside clock.

One a.m., three a.m. and still Dick was not home. Her ears were pricked for the sound of an engine but nothing disturbed the still night air. No phone call had come.

At first light, she hurried from the bed and ran downstairs to her office in case there was an email from Dick. Her in-box was empty and the monitor's bright but lifeless face taunted her. Wouldn't he have left a note if he had decided to fly the coop? Chloe shivered and put on the kettle to make some coffee. Outside, car headlights flooded the dining room and she raced to the window but it was a car doing a U-turn in the street. Still her headache lingered.

Curled up on the settee, her hands cradled the hot coffee. She would not wait any longer.

'Yes, I want to report a missing person.'

'And just who might this person be?'

'My husband. He wasn't here when I returned home from a meeting. I haven't seen him since. Yes, I understand that for someone to be missing it has to be forty-eight hours, but I'm worried. It's not like him. Oh, I didn't think to look. Hang on a minute.'

Chloe went out into the darkness, still holding her mobile phone. The garage was empty. She finished giving details to the on-duty policeman, who told her not to worry and that Richard would probably turn up soon. Chloe was not reassured. She felt panicky. She didn't want the marriage to end this way.

Chloe opened the blinds in the kitchen. Her eyes squinted involuntarily at the pale dawn. A few birds were starting their early morning song. Everything was just as it should be for this time of the morning, except in her house. Except that her husband was missing. Going through her mind, she tried to remember if she had been unkind; she often spoke her mind. Had she been out too much since she had become involved with the Universal Christian Women's Movement? Was her spiritual journey evolving at the expense of her marriage? Well, she had to do something to stay sane. Questions floated from her mind out into the chill air of the kitchen and hung there unanswered. She didn't expect him to retire from her life altogether.

Her thoughts of near guilt were interrupted by the buzzing of her mobile phone as it jumped around on the kitchen bench. *Richard! Something has happened. This'll be the police.*

'Oh, Chloe dear – just confirming that you will be at the extra meeting on Wednesday night.'

Get off the phone, Chloe muttered beneath her breath.

'Yes. I'll be there. Wouldn't miss it, Eleanor. Got to go – soup boiling over.' She pressed End Call.

A note. He must have left a note and she had overlooked it – some clue as to his whereabouts, some sign as to why he had just disappeared. Before dressing, she feverishly searched the bedroom for a note. Perhaps he'd put one under the pillow. Earlier, in the honeymoon days of their marriage, they would often leave little billets-doux under their respective pillows and, upon reading them, would giggle and then make passionate love. But there was no note.

Chloe threw her shoes at the wardrobe, her patience and plausible explanations exhausted. 'How dare he? How dare he treat me like this?' she screamed before throwing herself down on the bed, sobbing, punching at the beige duvet until the tears had dried up and she lay moaning about the unfairness of it all! *Damn Richard! Typical!* It was just like him to disappear to who knows where without a word; without any hint that anything could be wrong.

But as Chloe calmed down, she remembered that there was something terribly wrong, as past discussions had revealed. Why didn't he warn her that he was going somewhere? He could have had the decency to tell her he was leaving, surely. She felt the anger rising again, muttering about responsibility, anxiety, grief, fairness, anything that came to her mind. She felt the tears welling up again and fought them back. She wanted to stay mad. She wanted to stay angry. She wanted to blame him for it all; for the nights when he just wouldn't talk; for the nights when he talked too much and she couldn't get a word in; for the weekends when he would just mope about the house and not be interested in going out with her; for the numerous evening meals eaten in silence. Well, if this was how he was going to handle their relationship, their marriage, so be it. It would be on his head.

Chloe splashed her face, examined the puffy eyes and the tired hair that framed her once pretty face. *You look disgusting!* she muttered to the mirror. *You certainly are not the fairest of them all at the moment.*

Perhaps she shouldn't have gone to so many of those damn

meetings but at least there were people there who would communicate with her. Why couldn't he have taken an interest in her life for once? There were many, many times when she could swear that he tuned out deliberately as if he wished he were somewhere else. Well, bloody hell, he was somewhere else now and he could stay there as far she was concerned. No point in going over and over what had happened in the past. Not now.

A chill breeze swept suddenly stirred the curtains and shutting the window, Chloe fancied she saw a movement in the garden below but a second look revealed nothing.

Her first action the following morning was to double check if Richard's car was there. No harm in making sure. Perhaps last night she was too upset to really take notice. Slamming the front door hard behind her, Chloe walked quickly to the garage and aimed the remote control. The door responded slowly to reveal his car. She was absolutely positive that it hadn't been here the night before. Yet here it was, dirty as usual, sitting smugly beside her immaculate vehicle. She instinctively put out a hand to touch the bonnet and recoiled immediately. It was warm. Now that was impossible. Wasn't it? Could he have returned without her noticing? She retraced her steps inside the house, calling his name. No sound, no noise of a footfall on the staircase. The house was empty. If he was in some kind of trouble, he would contact her. She shivered involuntarily. Perhaps he was dead and she had just walked over his grave.

It was eleven-thirty and the morning sun was just gathering a little warmth as it began to flood the kitchen. Chloe shivered but this time it was because she was cold and anxious. She poured herself a strong measure of whiskey, closing her eyes and cradling the warming alcohol in her chilled hands, half wishing that she could disappear too away from all the anxieties in her life.

The police had now put out an official missing persons bulletin.

When Tuesday night rolled around, she wondered if she had the energy to go the meeting at Universal Christian Women's. She really would have preferred to stay home just in case… *Just in case what?* she asked herself. If she didn't go, they would think she wasn't serious about her commitment. On the other hand, it might cheer her up being with like-minded souls. She would go tonight and perhaps find some solace for her tormented spirit. Surely someone there would be able to advise and help her for she felt beyond trying to help herself. She wondered if she was beginning to lose it. Summoning all her strength, she went upstairs to the bathroom.

The bedroom felt unusually warm, although no sun ever reached the room even in summer. And what was that smell? A kind of perfume and yet nothing that was familiar at all, certainly not a fragrance she wore. She sniffed again. No, not perfume but rather a herbal smell, a bit like the incense she remembered in a Catholic church she had once visited on one of her many investigations for spiritual peace. She shuddered and the smell disappeared as quickly as it had arrived. Under the shower, Chloe washed herself slowly and thoughtfully cleansing her body of any negative vibration. She took some more analgesics to banish the stubborn headache.

The meeting hall was in near darkness.

Chloe called out, 'Anyone there? It's Chloe.'

A light suddenly flared its brightness.

'We're here. We're all here but we thought you weren't coming tonight. You are late.'

Chloe peered in the direction of the voice. 'Only by a few minutes.'

'Then come and sit – we've already started.'

Chloe felt a little chastised but sat. A chant started, one she'd never heard before. She adjusted her cloak, pulled the hood further over her head so her eyes were shielded from the accusing glances coming from the other hooded women. The feeling of hostility towards her was palpable and she couldn't understand why. Perhaps it was an anniversary of someone passing over; perhaps they were remembering a spirit long gone and who had a command over the assembled group, more in number than usual. She had only missed one meeting. What could happen or change in a week? The chanting had begun in a monotone but now was rising to a more high-pitched sound. Arms were lifting and waving as bodies swayed to the rhythm. The sway became a rocking, feet following with a soft tapping that increased to a stamping. Chloe followed as best she could but was becoming frightened now as the stamping escalated. The chanting turned to a screaming pitch now and the group sounded more like bats preparing for a feasting.

She sensed a danger but couldn't quite make out why; there was something inhuman about this behaviour. Without trying to attract attention, she began to slide along the row until she reached the aisle. She put one foot out but before she could follow it with the other foot, a cold, chill blanket of air enveloped her. She shivered and tried to move forward but she was fixed like a statue on a plinth. Wanting to cry out, she found that her voice had become mute, her vocal chords frozen in mid-scream. And then, then just as she feared she would choke, she lost consciousness.

6

Chloe felt the rush of cold wind on her face. If this was a dream, she wanted badly to wake up. Her fingers were frozen, her clothes inadequate for wherever this journey was taking her. There were no other sensations. She tried to open her eyes but they were shut fast. She heard nothing except the whooshing wind carrying her along beyond her control. She'd read about lucid dreaming but this was ridiculous. She wanted to wake up.

Suddenly, but almost pleasantly, she felt a warmth upon her eyelids, then on her cheeks. The warmth began to ripple down her entire body. Her eyes flickered and began to open. Blinking several times, she was now wide awake, holding up her hands to protect her eyes from bright sunlight. Nothing around her was recognisable. This wasn't even her town, she was sure. In fact, she could not even see any houses at all, let alone an apartment block that looked familiar. She looked down. Her feet were hovering about fifteen inches above the ground and she wore black boots that laced up to her lower calves. Panicking, she kicked her legs hard, trying to get them to make contact with the ground. Finally, her toes touched terra firma. All about her were fields under cultivation. Was it corn? Where in the hell was she?

Her ears picked up the distant sound of a flute but she couldn't recognize the tune. With the back of her hand, she wiped off the perspiration beading on her forehead. A drop fell onto the camisole she was wearing atop a long dun-coloured skirt slightly fraying at the hem. Despite the growing warmth of the sun, she shivered and reached for the thin woollen shawl about her shoulders. What had happened to her other clothes, the ones she had been wearing during the day? A million questions buzzed around in her head. She felt an indescribable fear surging in her belly, as voices in the distance signalled people were coming. Her fear instinctively led her into a calming chant she had learned to lessen the terror she felt rising to her throat. She closed her eyes, trying to blot out the sound of the voices. They couldn't be real. Nothing was real. But the throb of angry voices grew louder.

She opened her eyes. They were coming towards her and they weren't looking too friendly. They were dressed in peasant clothes much like her own. She called out tentatively and raised a hand. All heads turned towards her but to her dismay, they shouted some obscenities in her direction. They were cursing her and her terror increased as she heard the words more clearly now.

'Witch! Witch! Get her! She's a witch. She has been talking witch words. Witch!' The shouts became louder.

Fighting panic, Chloe began to run. She stumbled at first then took up speed and ran like the wind until she found herself threading her way through the stalks of corn in the field, feeling the pricking of the corn through her thin skirt. Beyond the corn was a country track and she ran towards it, looking behind to see the menacing little group some distance away. Thank God for her training as a runner. But she didn't stop. She must follow the track and perhaps it might take her to a town where she could get help.

She began to pant but just as she was about to despair at ever getting anywhere, a small, quaint cottage appeared on the horizon. The thatched roof hung low over the cottage walls, vegetables were growing in the front garden and to the side of the house two cows were grazing.

She knocked as loudly as she could on the solid wooden door. When she heard footsteps in the distance, she sighed with relief.

'Who be knocking now?.

The door flung open revealing a stout man with britches and a waist-coat.

'Please,' Chloe began, trying to slow her breathing. 'Please can you help me? I don't know where I am and I need to get in touch with my friend. I'm being chased by some people and I don't know what to do. Do you have a phone I could use?'

The stout man stood, mouth open. He suddenly went white and

began yelling. 'We don't want your sort here. Ye be gone afore I take a pitchfork to your hide. We don't want none of your wicked magic here.' He slammed the door in Chloe's face.

Chloe was more than puzzled. She was astounded first by the man's rudeness when a damsel in distress was asking for help, secondly by his threats. Just what sort was she? She just wanted some help and some answers to this ridiculous situation. If this was still a dream, well, thank you very much, I should like to wake up now. Frowning, she turned, running back to the track only to be nearly run down by a cart pulled by a couple of heavy horses.

'Hey, watch where you're going,' she instinctively yelled, as she tripped on a rut and nearly fell down.

'And you, you wicked excuse for a woman. What might you be doing here alone and trying to cause trouble for some honest country folk? Begone with you. Take your wickedness somewhere else.' The driver cracked his whip and urged his horses on.

Surely he must be mistaking her for someone else. Confused and very tired, Chloe continued running, following the cart at a distance in the hope that it would lead her to a town and some civilisation. She looked over her shoulder but there was no sign of her pursuers.

By the time Chloe arrived at the edge of the small village, she was exhausted and hungry. The village looked like a medieval movie set. A sign that read 'Pig and Whistle' swung outside a tavern. She entered.

'Hey! You can't come in here,' yelled the man behind the bar. 'Off you go now. Out. Out!'

'But,' Chloe began and got no further.

Two men came towards her and bodily lifted her up by the arms and swung her out the door.

She picked herself up from the dusty street and looked about. A few people pretended they had seen nothing. No one offered any help.

She walked up to one young woman and tried to engage her in conversation. 'Please, miss. Can you help me? I'm looking for somewhere to eat. I'm very hungry and I've travelled a great distance.'

There was fear on the girl's face, but she drew Chloe aside into a doorway. 'I don't know who you are or where you're from, but you can't just go into a tavern like that. It's not done,' she whispered. 'You'd better be on your way before you get into trouble.'

'I'm not looking for any trouble. What is this place anyway? I was chased by some people who kept yelling that I was a witch! Are they mad or what? I've never seen a place so, well, so backward either. I'm no more a witch than the Queen of England. Anyone would think this was back in the 1700s.'

Chloe watched the puzzled look on the girl's face as she replied slowly and deliberately.

'Well, that's because it is. I would say that you are the one out of kilter here. You appear out of nowhere, not knowing where you are and not knowing how to go about anything. I think I should be the one asking questions. It is not safe for someone like you to be wandering at large like this. Not safe at all. You had better get back to where you came from before they come for you.'

Chloe looked stunned. 'Come for me? What do you mean, I'm not safe? I'm English like you and have rights as a woman.'

'Not in these here parts, you don't, and like I say, it's women like you who give us other women a bad name. Now, I can't help you. Just warning you, that's all.' She leaned into Chloe and whispered softly, 'There's a stable out the back where you might take shelter for the night but don't stay longer than you have to. Now leave and quickly.' The girl slipped out of the doorway and hurried away.

Chloe was more confused than ever. Either she was going mad or already was mad. But she was frightened enough to heed the girl's warning and, placing her thin shawl over her head, she blended into the crowd.

7

The stable was deserted except for an old horse. She spoke to him but he must have been deaf because he barely looked up. He was such a bag of bones it was a wonder he could stand at all. Chloe opened the stable door and crept in, shutting the door carefully behind her. There was just enough room for her to curl up in one corner behind a mound of straw, and a casual glance into the stable would reveal nothing. The old horse wheezed loudly and the stench of the stable was disgusting but it was only horse dung and she could cope with that. She eventually slipped into a fitful sleep, memories of her grandfather's horses passing in and out of her exhausted brain.

A loud whinny woke Chloe. Holding her breath, she peered into the early morning mist to see what had disturbed the horse.

'Now there, old fella, settle down. I've brought thee some carrots which mouldy as they are will help fill your belly.'

The voice sounded kind enough. Should she take a chance and reveal herself. She decided to wait. The lad of about nineteen stroked the neck of the old nag and continued to talk to him while feeding the carrots. Chloe would have killed for a carrot. She was absolutely starving.

She heard a break in the lad's voice, followed by a sob. He rested his capped head on the horse's neck and wept.

Chloe was moved enough to speak. 'Excuse me. Please don't be concerned. I needed somewhere to sleep for the night and your horse seemed like good company.' She stood up as she spoke and the lad straightened and was obviously startled.

'What are ye doing here?' he said, wiping his eyes with a dirty sleeve. 'No one's allowed in the stable except me and me master.'

'Please don't be frightened. I mean no harm. I'm very lost and don't know where to turn next.'

'You're certainly not from around here, are ye?'

'Well, no. You won't tell anyone, will you?' Chloe moved a little closer. 'I'm not sure just how I got here but now that I am, I need some help. Do you know where I might find some work and lodging?'

'Well, I'm surprised that you don't have, you know, some easy work,' he chortled.

'What do you mean, some easy work?'

'Well, what a woman of your sort does, doesn't she? I mean, there be lots of men who would bed thee for a crown, if you're lucky.'

'Bed me!' Chloe recoiled in horror. 'I'm not a prostitute! I am not one of those women at all. I am a…' She stopped, not knowing just what she really was at all. '…a traveller,' she finished.

'And where might ye be travelling to? A woman alone, with no chattels, no money, no work. A bit strange, if you ask me. But I won't tell. I don't need any more problems.'

'I noticed you were upset a minute ago. Because of the horse?' Chloe asked.

'Well, I'm not ashamed. This horse and me are like two halves of a coin, we are. Been tending 'im since he came here and now…now they want to send him to the knackery and I just can't bear it.'

'Well, he's old and a bit wheezy but he's still got a keen eye and he likes you, I can tell.'

'How can you tell?'

'Animals let you know when they like you. I've got a dog, well, had a dog and that's how he was with me. Can't you take him away somewhere with you? If they're going to send him off, they won't miss him, will they?' Chloe's eyes began to mist over as she thought of Andy and how she chastised him for his barking. She was surprised that she remembered him when her past was so elusive that she couldn't recall anything else. What she wouldn't give now to have him by her side.

'More than my life's worth.' The lad hung his head.

Chloe had an idea. 'Well, what if we go together? You and me. You know the countryside and together we could cover a bit of distance before he's missed, or you for that matter. We can help each other.' Chloe caught the shine of hope in the lad's eye.

'Ooh, I don't know, really I don't, but I can't live without Harry. He's all I've got.'

'Well, then. Let's give it a go. We can take it in turns to ride him. Come on, it's not quite light yet. We have time but only if we go now.'

Two shadowy figures stole out of the stable, leading Harry, and by the time it was light, they had cleared the town.

'I suppose you've got a name,' she asked the lad.

'It's Pippin. Pippin the Younger.' He smiled shyly.

'Pleased to make your acquaintance, Pippin the Younger. Mine's Chloe.' She could have added 'the elder' but thought better of it.

The sun shone down warmly for the best part of the day. The track was mainly used by farmers, Pippin had explained, and indeed, they passed a few. Chloe stayed close to the horse and was shadowed by his bulk. By about three o'clock, Chloe guessed as she gazed heavenwards, she was tired.

'We can stop a while under yon tree,' suggested Pippin. Harry seemed pleased to be able to graze. Pippin miraculously produced a crust of bread from his pocket. Chloe felt drowsy after she had eaten and felt like closing her eyes, but she forced them to stay open. She looked upwards through the broad-leafed tree and noticed something flapping on the tree trunk. Curiously, she stood up and read what appeared to be a notice nailed crudely to the tree.

Reward offered for apprehension of any witch found at large. The scratching process will be enforced to determine the guilt of said witch.
Signed: Witchfinder General

Chloe gasped. She quickly reached up and tore the notice from the tree before Pippin could see it, although she doubted he could read. But there was a rough drawing of what folk appeared to think a witch looked like. The drawing looked remarkably like Chloe. She felt her heart leap. Somewhere on their journey she must try and find some clothing that looked less witchlike.

'Pippin dear, do you think we should be moving on? T'would be nice to find some shelter afore nightfall and we do have a larger member as well to keep hidden.'

'Right you are, miss. Let's be off then.'

Harry was reluctant to leave good fodder but he allowed Pippin to gently lead him on. He trusted his master implicitly and if he wanted to leave, then there was a good reason.

Chloe walked in silence, deep in thought. The scrunched-up poster wriggled in her pocket and she shuddered a little. She was no more a witch than Harry and she suppressed a giggle in spite of her forebodings.

'Pippin,' she finally began, 'Pippin, have you ever met a witch?'

'Can't say I have, miss. I've heard tell of 'em, though. Why, my own master had some nasty dealings with one. She said, I have heard, that she could cure his sick wife with some magic herbs. Well, the wife didn't get cured and there was hell to pay. My master accused the herb woman of being a witch and a whole lot of townsfolk gathered around to see. The Witchfinder General was summoned and he did that scratching test I've heard tell of. Well, it appeared that the woman didn't bleed and it was pronounced that she was a witch.' Pippin stopped.

'Well, do go on, Pippin. What happened then?'

'Well, first they chopped off her hands and then, then she was burned to death. I've been told the screamings were enough to wake the devil himself.'

Chloe felt faint. It just sounded so, so medieval. But then, here she was in a time not of her choosing, a long way from all things remembered, and from people she knew and loved. Tears began to prick her eyes. 'My goodness, Pippin. What a dreadful story. You don't think that still happens, do you?'

'Couldn't say, miss. But it don't make no difference to me and you. We're just travellers going, going…well, just where are we going, miss? Makes no sense just to be awandering through the countryside. We can't just do this forever. And besides,' Pippin looked worried, 'old Harry here can't keep on walking forever. He needs a place to stay and live out his old age.'

'You're absolutely right, Pippin. I say we keep on going until we reach the next town and then see if there's some work I could do for someone. I've had a good education, so it shouldn't be too hard to find some sort of employment. Then with the money, we can rent a small cottage with a little plot of land and put Harry out to pasture.' This was more a dream than a reality but she wanted to be positive for her own sake as well as for Pippin.

'What's ejucation, miss? Pippin enquired.

'Oh, well, it's…well, it's learning about things – going to a school and studying. Have you ever been to school, Pippin?'

'Only rich folks go to school. Me mum and dad died in a terrible sickness and I've been on me own since. I had a sister for a while, but she ran off with a soldier and I haven't seen her since.'

'But how have you managed to live? Where did you stay?'

'Wherever I could and I would sweep out stables and be allowed to sleep with the horses. You get used to it really.' Pippin grinned. 'I'll bet you never slept with horses in a stable.'

'You'd be right, although who knows where I'll end up? Come on, let's hurry on a bit. We want to be off the road before dark.'

8

Fierce sniffed the air. There was a storm brewing and the horses knew it was coming before anyone else. With a quick, fluid movement, Fierce was at the side of Flare, her sleek black Friesian mare. Since a foal, Flare had been raised kindly and gently and now he was as soft as butter. In a crisis, his steel was there and Fierce could rely on him totally – they matched each other strength for strength.

The others were drawing about their wagons as the skies darkened, calling the little ones to come, and as the heavens opened and pelted down the torrents of rain, pots of soup were snatched from the camp fire embers and taken inside.

Fierce stroked her mare, nuzzled her and whispered into her ear. 'It's only a storm. You've been through this dozens of times, my love. Now, hold still. It will be over soon.'

Flare pawed the ground but not in fear or anger. He understood the calming words of his mistress. He nickered softly, calling out to the other horses in the camp not to be afraid.

Fierce tore a large chunk of the stale bread, broke it into bite-size pieces and plunged into the pot. She would not be sharing her dinner with her man this night. Nor would she any other night. He was long gone and she pined for him with an ache beyond describing. The nights were long and empty and the days not much better as she plied the fruits of her craft at the near and distant markets, sometimes only bringing in enough coins to buy a few turnips and some dark, rye bread.

This night she wove the bright, thick strands into braids that would become halters. Each one took several days – harvesting the tough reeds, dyeing them with vegetable juices, hanging them to dry before being satisfied that the rope was to her strict standard. The dye would give off pungent odours and passers-by from the villages would sniff the air, look suspiciously over the field fences in the hope of spying the Gypsy witch and her cauldron, and call her names.

'Go back to your tribe, witch!'

'How much are you charging for your evil potions?'

'What spell will you cast on yourself to make you disappear?'

Fierce heard but tried to ignore the taunts which had become part of living as they moved around the country. Her long, coal black hair fuelled the myth further. Village children skipping along the rutted roads sang rhymes about witches and their britches and then ran like the furies were after them in case the witch saw them and gave chase on her powerful horse with the flaring nostrils and long, black mane.

The coloured halters were popular. There were some who looked upon them as witch magic and wouldn't buy, but the men – oh yes, the men with their sly looks and greasy palms – would buy. On slack days, Fierce would tell fortunes, reassuring the women that their husbands would treat them kindly, or perhaps on other days, she would see a handsome, blond stranger come into their dreary lives. How they would blush and titter behind their gloved hands. Fierce would watch as they clustered about each other afterwards to compare the 'tellings'. All this amused her and she made a little extra money as well.

When the rumours began, quietly, surreptitiously at first then building, not so many came to have their fortune told. Husbands would grab the elbows of their wives and hurry them past the stall where the bright halters swung in the breeze and the emerald green curtain swayed, revealing just a glimpse of the telling ball at rest on its little table.

The first wash of dawn woke Fierce, pushing itself cheekily through the parted curtains of the wagon. She yawned, sat up and looked at the fresh green of the field. With the rising sun, the earth began to warm, a gentle ground mist hovered and in the near distance, she could make out the breath fog from the horses as they stood patiently waiting for their morning hay. Spring was rippling through the air and the subtle smell of daffodils wafted over the camp. As the mist lifted, activity began with the lighting of fires for the breakfast gruel.

Fierce drew in a deep breath. She had slept well enough and she would not be eating gruel today. A strong brew of tea would suffice with the bread left over from the night before. She had hopes of selling many halters before the day ended.

Flare was waiting and while he ate, she gave him a quick brushing and threw the rug across his broad back. As she secured one of the bridles, Flare whinnied and moved about restlessly as she hoisted the bundle of halters across his withers before swinging herself up. They were off and out the gate before the rest of the camp had finished breakfast. She urged Flare to a gallop and they were soon racing down the country track in perfect synchrony with one another.

9

'No, miss,' Pippin was saying. 'I don't think this is a good idea, you going to a market. There be lots of folk there and you might be recognised.' Pippin had a look of concern about his young features.

'Oh no, Pippin. Quite the contrary. I will blend in and how could anyone possibly recognise me as I'm not from around here? It will be perfectly safe. I promise,' Chloe added, smiling reassuringly at Pippin, who did not look convinced at all. 'Come, perhaps I could find some work. I'm good at sewing.'

'Sewing, miss?' Pippin questioned. 'What would you be sewing around here?'

'Well, people have to wear clothes and if I can get some material, I could make some dresses for the ladies who shop at the markets.'

'Oh, and how are you going to get the materials to do that? You have no money and I certainly can't help you.'

'Pippin, don't be so negative.' Chloe was beginning to get irritated. 'Maybe one of the stallholders will let me work and earn some money that way. I'm good at selling too.'

'That's as maybe, but I don't know.' Pippin shook his head.

'Look! There's a large field. Perhaps we could leave Harry tethered there, look! Just under that tree. There's no one around and all horses look the same. No one would notice him anyway. Come on, Pippin. I'll open the gate.'

Reluctantly, Pippin led Harry through the gate. 'I suppose he will be glad of a rest and there's some nice fresh grass under the tree. There, Harry, me boy, we'll be back before you can say neigh!'

'My, you have quite a sense of humour, don't you, Pippin?'

'Do I, miss? Well, it helps to have a bit of a laugh, don't it?'

'Yes, it surely does. Now, quickly, let's be off. Away to the market and may we be blessed with some good fortune this day.' Chloe couldn't help notice that she was beginning to pick up Pippin's vernacular – perhaps a good thing as she wanted to be unnoticed. She smiled to herself. It was hardly likely that she would run into one of her next-door neighbours from back in her past. Or a friend for that matter. She felt confident and strode along the rutted lane with a lightness in her step, Pippin following close behind.

Chloe fingered the rough material lying on the rough wooden bench which served as a counter. Woven baskets lay next to the material, funny-looking small dolls made from what could only have been straw. They looked just like mini scarecrows. Within minutes, several women were queuing. A rather harassed seller was becoming quite flustered.

Chloe, feeling braver than she perhaps should, cleared her throat. 'Scuse me, but would you like me to help? I have had some experience selling.'

'Suit yerself. I could do with a bit. Ta.' She threw a quick look in Chloe's direction. She was too busy to ask questions.

By lunchtime, there were very few items left for sale.

'Thanks, miss, for your help. I've not been well lately and nearly didn't come this morning but I needed the money. Me husband's away looking for work. But you have been so kind and I must give you a few coins for your trouble.'

Chloe held up her hand. 'No, that's not necessary. I was happy to help. Anyway, I'm sure you have children to feed as well as your husband.'

The girl looked down. 'Not any more. Two little girls I had, seven and nine. They was taken by the great mortality last winter.' Tears formed in her eyes.

'I'm so sorry.' Chloe put her hand gently on the woman's arm. 'What's your name?'

'Lily,' she whispered. 'I miss them terribly. You have bairns?'

'No, I haven't.'

'Anyways, that's life, isn't it? But I want you to have just a few coins for your help. Truly it was such luck that you came along.' Lily scrutinised Chloe. 'You're not from these parts, are you?

'No. I'm, er, travelling through. I have a young lad with me for a bit of protection, I guess. He's only about nineteen, my nephew in fact. His mother is poorly so he's travelling with me, looking for some work.'

'Do you think you might stay for a bit here, in this town? You could work for me a bit longer, just so as I can get me fitness back again.' She looked almost beseechingly at Chloe. 'And your nephew, he could ask at the blacksmith at the end of the town if he needs a worker. It's worth a try.'

'I would love to help you out too. I have fallen on hard times lately and as long as the weather holds, we can sleep in an empty field. I just need a few coins to purchase some food. Thank you. I'll tell Pippin. He was here earlier, but I guess he's wandered off to look at things. I'll find him and come back, all right?'

Lily nodded.

'Pippin! Pippin!' Chloe caught up with him. 'Good news, look!' She held out her hand holding the coins. 'And Lily said you might try the blacksmith at the end of town. He could be looking for help. It looks as if our prospects might change for the better.'

Pippin looked sullen. 'And who's Lily?'

'She owns one of the stalls.'

'Oh, but it don't change nothing if I can't find somewhere for Harry to rest. And what about winter? He will need some shelter. Them coins won't go far at all.'

'Well, Lily has asked me to help her some more. That means more coins. Don't you see? Our luck is changing.'

Her optimism wasn't rubbing off on Pippin.

'And I ain't no way taking charity from a woman. It just isn't right.'

'Look, these are hard times. And just so as you know, I told a little white lie and said you were my nephew. So now that we're related, it will be all right to share the money, won't it? Won't it?' she emphasised.

'You are wicked,' Pippin let a small conspiratorial smile play on his lips. 'I suppose we'll be partners then. I'll come with you to the blacksmith.'

Lily was packing up when they returned to her stall. 'Shall I see you next Wednesday, then? Got to make hay while the sun shines. It'll soon be winter. And mind how you go, young Pippin. You are lucky to have an aunt like Chloe here.'

'I am.' Pippin lowered his eyes.

Another stall was finishing for the day.

Chloe stopped briefly to admire the colourful halters hanging from a hook on a post. 'These are lovely.' She looked at the tall, dark girl behind the counter. 'Did you make them?

'Yes I did, and if you don't mind, I'm in a hurry. She lowered her glance and began to take down the halters. 'If you want to buy, you'll have to come back next week.'

'Oh, no I don't want to buy. I haven't any money. Yet,' she added. 'Perhaps I shall come next week.' Chloe didn't mention that she would be helping out a fellow stall holder.

The blacksmith's hammer could be heard long before they reached the smithy. Chloe and Pippin stood at a small distance, waiting for him to look up which he did almost immediately.

He mopped his very red and hot face with a kerchief, raised his eyebrows and spoke. 'What would you be wanting? I don't see no horse.'

He didn't seem unfriendly so Chloe nudged Pippin. 'If you please, sir, would you be needing any help at all? I am looking for a bit of work.'

The blacksmith smiled at being called sir. 'Well, now what experience have you had, eh?'

'I've spent most of me life around horses and I understand them as if I was one meself. I have done a bit of smithy work too and I have shod not a few horses.' Pippin drew a breath.

'My all that and in one so young.' The blacksmith smiled, pausing from hammering but still pumping the bellows with a long wooden handle.

'I'm nineteen,' Pippin replied indignantly as he watched, awestruck. The huffing of the forge and the clanging of metal on metal hissing and spitting fired his imagination. He could have been in a dragon's den or under a mountain with magical swords and dwarves. The white-hot fire, necessary for forging the iron, was almost blinding and Pippin could feel its strong heat.

'Nineteen, eh? Well as a matter of fact, I could do with a little help. Can't take you on full time, you understand, but it just so happens that my usual boy is poorly at the moment. You could fill in for him. Would that do? Oh, by the way, my name's Oliver.' He smiled and looked searchingly at Chloe, who was standing back. 'And you would be...'

'I'm Pippin's aunt. His family is very unwell and can't afford to feed him so I said I'd take him with me on my travels. I, too, am looking for work but not here.' She blushed.

'No. Do you have any skills?'

'Well, I can read and write a little and I can sew very well...' Chloe didn't want to divulge the extent of her education right now.

'Well, I'm sure you will find something.'

'I am hopeful. For a little while I shall be helping Lily at the market.'

'Yes, poor girl. She has had some hard times. Lost her bairns, she did. Now, young man, can you come by tomorrow morning at about six?'

'Six? Why, I surely can. I always rise early to tend to Harry. Thank you, sir.' He beamed.

'Harry?'

'Me horse. He's old but he's just the most faithful friend and we go everywhere together. There's some that would send him to the knackers and he ain't ready for that. And neither am I,' Pippin said fiercely.

'Your loyalty is to be commended.' Oliver smiled, raising his blackened hand in salute. 'Tomorrow then?'

Pippin and Chloe went to retrieve Harry, who was napping under the very large oak tree.

'We must find a stream for Harry so he can drink. And so we can too.'

Fresh running water was safe enough. Otherwise, folk, mainly the rich, would drink beer, ensuring that they wouldn't be poisoned by the water from the town pumps. Gin was a popular drink too, coming from far away Holland. Pippin had never had either. Chloe had a remembrance of a time, long ago, when she used to be partial to gin but in what way she couldn't recall.

The travelling threesome went in search of water and a safe field wherein to spend the night.

Suddenly, from out of the descending gloom behind them, there was a thundering of hooves and a figure on a large Friesian horse sped past them, so close that Chloe felt the rider's garment brush her cheek.

She drew back, almost falling. 'That was a close one. Obviously horses have the right of way here,' she exclaimed.

'Well, of course they do. If you get in the way, that's just too bad. Why, nearly every week someone gets skittled.' Pippin looked at her in surprise. 'You didn't know that?'

'No, I didn't!' Chloe replied crossly. 'That reckless rider could have killed me!'

'Best to be on the lookout then, miss. Stick to the side of the road.'

'You call this a road? It's nothing more than a country track and a poorly maintained one at that.'

Pippin just looked puzzled. She really was a strange one. What life had she been leading before their paths crossed?

Chloe yawned and her feet began to drag. Darkness began to close in about them and it was getting colder.

In the distance, Pippin spied the tiny glow of a fire in a field. As they approached, the glow widened and he could just make out figures clustered around it.

'I think they may be Gypsies, though, so there's no guarantee that we will be made welcome,' Pippin whispered to Chloe. 'But we can try.' Pippin nudged at the gate, which gave. 'You stay here while I investigate.'

He left them on the outside of the gate, closed it carefully and walked slowly but deliberately towards the little group. He was immediately noticed. Sharp, they were.

'Hey, boy. Don't you know you're trespassing? This is our field. Get out before I set the dogs on you!'

Two large dogs with yellow eyes were tethered to a coloured wagon.

'I mean no harm, please, sir. I am simply looking for a friendly place for my aunt and horse to rest for the night. We will be no trouble.' Pippin was well aware that lots of Gypsies trespassed themselves and he stood his ground. 'We've as much right to this field as you and we are not many as you can see.' He gestured to where Harry and Chloe were standing just beyond the gate.

At this point, the door from another wagon flung open and a tall girl appeared. Her long black hair swung in the rising wind and she looked Pippin up and down then cast her eyes in the direction of Chloe and Harry. The horse looked half dead and it was obvious that the travellers, if that's what they were, were very weary. The girl looked familiar.

'That's enough, Waldo,' she spat at the man. 'They look harmless. It's not going to hurt us any to take them in just for the one night. Where are your manners?' She walked over to Pippin. 'What's your name, lad? And who be these stragglers here hiding behind the gate like robbers?'

'I'm called Pippin and they are no stragglers nor robbers. Chloe is my aunt and I call the horse Harry.'

The girl threw back her head and roared with laughter. 'Harry! Harry! Such a foolish name for a horse. He looks half dead to me anyway. I'm sure he won't eat much!' She laughed again.

'Yes, he's old but he's strong and we've been together for a very long time.'

Fierce softened a bit. She knew only too well the strength of a relationship with a horse. She motioned for Chloe and Harry to enter. 'Mind you shut the gate after you. I saw you at my stall this day.' She turned to Chloe with more interest than she had previously shown at the market.

'Yes, that was me all right. It's good of you to let us stay,' said Chloe. 'We're really weary and we won't be any trouble.'

'That you won't, I'll see to it,' Fierce muttered loudly enough for them to hear.

'We've brought our own food and we have water.' Chloe unwrapped the stale loaf of bread. 'We're more than willing to share with you.'

'Not necessary. You can tie up the old nag over there away from the other horses. Don't want them catching anything. And that tree over yonder has a very generous canopy which will shelter you from the weather and protect you from the sun – should you still be here tomorrow.' Fierce disappeared into her wagon, slammed the door.

The angry Waldo turned his back on them. Apparently, the girl was boss.

Chloe hoped they wouldn't be here tomorrow. But at least for the night they had a safe haven. She and Pippin huddled together, too tired to worry whether they were cold or not, Pippin muttering under his breath, 'Old nag indeed! I'll give her old nag, or should it be old hag?'

'Heard that, Pippin. Just be grateful we're safe. You can't blame her for being careful, and she's not an old hag. Why, she wouldn't be much older than me.'

'Gypsies are all the same. They don't trust anyone.'

Does anyone trust them? Chloe wondered, not having too much information about them. There were no internet cafés here.

Chloe awoke first, the smell of newly lit kindling in her nostrils. Her belly felt empty; they had decided to keep the bread for their first meal of the day. Someone had draped a coarse blanket over the two travellers. She let Pippin sleep and slid out from underneath the covering so as not to disturb him.

10

Fierce yawned, leapt from her bunk bed and dressed quickly. There were reeds to gather so she swallowed a cold cup of tea with a mouthful of bread and hurriedly left the wagon.

Crossing the field, she stopped at where Flare was tethered and ran her fingers through his long mane. She untied him and the two of them made their way to the stream that ran the perimeter of the land where they had been camping now for some months. Aware that they could be moved on at any time, she had to make the most of their stay here.

Flare drank thirstily. Fierce splashed some water onto her face, ran her fingers through her tresses and turned suddenly at the sound of a twig snapping.

Chloe hesitated then spoke. 'I just wanted to thank you for helping us last night, and for the blanket. It did get a bit cold.'

'So you'll be moving on, then?'

'Oh,' said Chloe, 'yes, I guess so. But not just yet as I have a little bit of work helping Lily at the market. You know her?'

'I know her. Works harder than that layabout husband of hers. She certainly doesn't stay with him for his money. Are you married?'

Chloe was taken aback by the direct question. 'Yes and no.'

'You have to be one or the other, so which?'

'My, er, husband disappeared and I haven't heard from him for a very long time, so that leaves me somewhere in between married and not married, I guess. He didn't like the things I like and was highly critical of my association with a spiritual group.' Chloe felt herself blush.

Fierce stiffened. 'You're not a witch, are you? Not that I've got anything against witches but they come to a very sticky end. Not many of them around these days. My mother was a witch. They killed her.'

'What? But what did she do that was so wrong?' asked Chloe

'She was a healer really and helped many of us heal from different ailments. She was also a Gypsy – not a good combination.' Fierce cupped her hand and drank from the bubbling stream.

'So she was killed because she helped people?'

'Ignorance is to blame. People go along with the popular thinking of the day, but they themselves don't think.'

'Well, I am sorry about your mother but I'm not a witch.'

'If you don't mind me saying, your clothing would beg otherwise.'

'Well, it's all I have. I arrived in this and had no say in it. Maybe that would explain why I wasn't allowed to enter the tavern,' Chloe said.

'People are still suspicious of strangers and you are pretty strange. You don't look like folks around here. They don't trust easily.'

'So it would appear. That man last night, he didn't like me.'

'Waldo doesn't like anyone. He doesn't like me much because I am the leader of our group and he is against women having any power at all.'

'Well, we won't stay. There might be another place we could be while I make enough money to feed us for a while before we move on. Pippin is going to the blacksmith's this morning to do some work. I had better rouse him. He mustn't be late.'

'Is Chloe your real name?'

'Yes.'

'It's pretty. And you and Pippin can stay here for a while. I'll soften up old Waldo. Now I must get busy picking these reeds. I need them to make the halters I sell at the market. Perhaps, once the reeds are dyed and dried, I could show you how to braid them.' Without waiting for a reply, Fierce took off up the bank of the stream, where Chloe could just discern a large clump of reeds.

Chloe pondered on Fierce's position of power in the camp. And her safety. Yes, she was strong, there seemed no doubt about that, but if her mother had been killed because she was considered a witch, then what about her daughter? Wouldn't she be under some suspicion? Granted, from what she'd picked up since she arrived here, Chloe knew that it wasn't a common practice any more to drown or burn witches but there were some ignorant trouble-stirrers, usually men who hated women and would draw on hysteria and superstition to further their cause whatever that may be. Back home they might have been called misogynists, but Chloe wasn't back home now and might never be again. She remembered the poster she'd seen attached to the tree she and Pippin had passed on the early part of their journey. She shuddered. Somehow she would have to find some clothing that wouldn't arouse suspicion. She could ask Fierce but felt a little intimidated by this dark-haired horsewoman who spoke her mind. She gave the impression that she was fearless. Was she? Questions bubbled up but now was not the time to search for answers.

Pippin had already stirred. Harry was munching on some grass near where he was tethered.

'Here,' offered Pippin. 'The lady left this for yer breakfast.'

Chloe took the rye bread and the piece of coarse country cheese. She was ravenous and wolfed it down. A long draught of water she had fetched from the stream followed the bread and as she stowed the mug in her carry all, she motioned to Pippin. 'We must be away, young Pippin. You've a job to go to and I must see about mine at the market.'

Harry was not to be hurried as the trio walked along the rutted lane towards the market square. Brambles hung across their path and more than once, Chloe's hair was caught in their thorny grasp. Pippin whistled a tuneless melody that was unrecognisable. He was lost in his own little world; probably thinking about his future.

The ping of hammer on anvil cut through the morning air with authority. They had arrived at the blacksmith's.

'Now then, young Pippin. Glad you have come. Set you down there and watch what I am doing so you get the gist of it all. You can tether yer 'orse over there by that yon tree.' He nodded in the tree's direction.

Pippin did as he was bid. He had butterflies in his stomach and his eyes flickered nervously from the smithy to the tree. He tethered Harry and went to sit on the piece of hewn log to watch the performance of the blacksmith. A huge bellows blew life into the coals of the fire. Pippin felt his forehead sweat even from where he sat so hot was the fire. He was in awe as the hammer flew, the sparks shot out from the anvil and a horse shoe began to take shape. When the shoe was considered finished, long heavy tongs were used to pick it up and plunge it into a malmsey butt full of water. It hissed, and steam rose from the collision between the two mediums before dispersing rapidly into the morning air.

Pippin noticed racks of mysterious-looking tools: hoes, shovels, plough points, axes, household tools for cooking, like forks and spoons, and many knives as well. A selection of files lay within easy reach of the blacksmith and the tongs hung close by to lift the shoes and transfer them to the butt of water. On a nearby bench lay a collection of nails. Pippin was fascinated and could only wonder at what job he would be given.

'Well, boy, what do you think? Would you like to become a blacksmith?' The smithy chuckled as he noticed the wide eyes of the boy.

'Well, I don't know. I just don't know if I could ever learn how to make all these things,' he gestured with his arm towards the hoes and other tools.

'Well, the knowledge don't come overnight, you know. Takes many years of being an apprentice first of all and then more years of experience before you can make a decent living out of it. I'm a very busy man, which is why I would like your help, and there are many, many horses who need shoes. And nails, special nails that attach the shoes to the hooves of the horses. Now, let's see. What can I give you to do that would help me.' He scratched the stubble on his double chin. 'See those shoes in a pile? Well, they have just been finished and I need them to be sorted into sizes. Do you think you could do that?

And put them in neat piles over there.' He pointed to a vacant corner of the shop.

Pippin could hardly see, it was so dark. The bellows hissed and the anvil sang its eerie tune as the smithy hammered.

'And after you've done that,' the smithy continued, 'you can sweep up any leftover bits of iron filings on the floor.'

'Yes, sir!' said Pippin quickly noticing a heavy bristled broom leaning against the wall.

All the while, Chloe looked on with quiet amusement at the scene playing out before her. 'Right then, Pippin. I'll leave you to your work and I'll be off to Lily's stall.'

11

Dick awoke to the sound of dishes clinking and muffled voices. For a mind-numbing minute, he was confused as to where he was until it came surging back into his still sleepy brain.

He had slept well enough and was hoping that the dream of his present condition would evaporate and he would be back in his own bed in Stoking-on-Trent. Looking about him as he rubbed his eyes, he knew that he was indeed still in old London Town and he wasn't dreaming at all. Once on his feet, he smoothed down his apparel and walked into the next room – it was the kitchen, and the kindly Mellie, whom he had met the evening before, was elbows deep in flour.

'Mornin',' she greeted him cheerfully. 'Trust you have slept well. The master's not up yet but there's tea abrewing over the fire and soon you will have some tasty hot muffins.'

Dick helped himself to the tea. 'Have you been here long, Mellie?' he asked her.

'Oh, aye. Years and years. I can hardly remember when I ain't been here with the master. He's good to me and he likes what I do. In the kitchen, that is,' she giggled, blushing.

'I understand.' Dick wanted to keep up the conversation to fill in the awkward silences between stranger and cook. 'And what about the master. Is he a good writer?'

'Can't say that I would know anything about that. I cook and clean. Had no ejucation myself much. Never learned to read neither. I come from a very poor family. My mother was always sick and her mother tried to heal her with herbs and potions but it didn't work and in the end, she died and I would have stayed with my grandmother but they took her away.'

'They?'

'Yes, the prosecutors. Said she was a witch and because my mother wasn't cured, she was blamed for her daughter's death. I never heard from her again. Folks say she was thrown into the river and drowned.'

'But that's dreadful. Do you mean to say that people really believed in witches to that extent?' Dick was incredulous.

'Oh yes, luvvy. Once the Witchfinder General tracked yer down, yer had no hope if he thought you were a witch and he could prove it.'

'How could he prove it?'

'He had his ways and I've heard tell they were terrible ways. That's all I know. I dare say the master knows a lot more, you know, with his brother being in the law and all.'

'Perhaps I'll ask him, then,' Dick replied, staring into his tea as if a genie would jump out. 'Good tea, Mellie.'

'Ta, sir. Now put your cup down on this table here and I'll butter you a nice hot muffin.'

'Good morning, Dick. I trust you slept well enough? Mmm! Muffins.' Henry beamed.

'Well enough. And thank you for putting me up. I've been chatting to Mellie and I'm about to try one of her delicious muffins.

'I will join you. She's a treasure, you know. Best muffins in all of London Town.' Henry poured himself a cup of tea and sat down on a chair near the fire. 'Bit chilly this morn, wouldn't you say, Dick?'

'I agree. I am so appreciative of you taking me in. I wouldn't have lasted a night out on the streets. Pretty frightening place to be after dark, I wager. Er, Henry, on the day I arrived here, not long before I bumped into you, I saw something rather disturbing.'

'Hm? And what was that, dear boy?'

'Well, I saw this kid, he couldn't have been more than six years old, nick an apple from a barrow. The owner chased him, and there they were slipping and sliding through the slimy muck from a butcher's stall. He was caught. The guy who owned the fruit stall was belting into him with this big, stout stick and in the excitement, the apple dropped in the mud and horse excrement. An old woman intervened, cursing the

fruit stall holder, telling him his apples were even too mouldy to give
her horse and to leave the boy alone. The boy was released, and ran off
as the man threatened him that things would be worse for him if he
ever did such a thing again. He was just a kid. Is this a common thing?'

'Ah yes,' Henry replied. A common enough incident for the
children who live by their wits. Our Robin Redbreasts largely ignore
them but it is still possible for a judge to sentence a felon to be hanged,
drawn and quartered. In practice, the sentence is always commuted to
hanging and decapitation.' He drew on his pipe, a frown creasing his
forehead.

'But that's awful. The commuted sentence is hanging and
decapitation? He was just a boy.' Dick shuddered. 'How many kids
live like that, uncared for, being treated like animals?'

'Dear boy,' Henry spoke seriously, 'do not distress yourself. There is
nothing to be done. We do what we can, and occasionally, one of these
waifs will be plucked from the street and taken in by a kindly family,
but that is rare…too, too rare, I'm afraid.'

'But where do these children sleep?'

'Where they can. In hidden crevices of buildings, in dark church
corners, sometimes in fields. They grow up on the streets and know
nothing else, having been cast out perhaps by drunken parents, or they
have simply run away, making their own decisions to live by their wits.
No one wants to help them. They are seen as filth, thieves who deserve
no better and who prey on people. And that they do. It is a way of life
foisted upon them. Unfortunately, their wits often let them down.'
Henry paused. 'And Dick, does this not happen in your, er, world to
some extent?'

'I'm afraid it does but not on such a grand scale and with less
cruelty. There are charities who provide food and sometimes shelter for
the homeless kids and there are more than most people would imagine.
I'm sure some steal and they form their own communities. They're
often introduced to drugs and alcohol at a very early age too.'

'Oh dear, then we have not come far at all dealing with unfortunates.

I am hoping, as well as improving our legal system, to draw up plans for an institution to care for vagabond children but I fear my ideas will be met with vigorous opposition. What do you think, as a man of the law?'

'In this climate, I would have to agree,' mused Dick. 'But who knows? Perhaps you will be able to change the course of history. One has to try.'

'My word, my word,' Henry affirmed. 'Now, try one of these hot buttered muffins. Mellie has a way with them.'

Almost reluctantly, Dick took one of the proffered muffins as Henry continued.

'Dick, I wonder if you would like to meet my brother later this morning so we can discuss thoughts about our new police enforcement plans. Just in their infancy, mind you, but something must be done.'

'Certainly. I'm ready when you are, Henry.' The muffin was getting stuck in his throat.

At nine-thirty, the streets were already bustling with London folk going about their various businesses. Dick kept tripping over the uneven cobblestones.

'It's a skill,' laughed Henry. 'You'll get used to them after a while. It's a bit like dancing and trying to avoid your partner's toes.'

'Never been much of a dancer.'

'Oh, here we are. John will be expecting me, but you will be a surprise and I'm sure he will be delighted to have a fellow law man to chat with.'

After a sharp knock with his cane, Henry didn't have to wait long before the large door swung open and his brother welcomed him with a strong hug.

'And who might this gentleman be?' he enquired, looking at Dick with some curiosity.

'Ah, you will be glad we came. This is Dick and he is from, er, well I can't quite remember where, but he is a lawyer.'

'You mean a magistrate, like me.'

'No, I mean a lawyer. Much advanced, I would gauge, for he speaks of things I know not. He might be able to help us, John.'

John stroked his small beard, looked over the top of his rimless glasses at Dick and cleared his throat. 'Not a member of the old Whittington family, are you, Dick?' He chortled, pleased with his little joke.

'No, I'm afraid not. Never learned to ride a horse.' Two brothers, same joke. Dick smiled to himself.

'Never mind. It's not necessary when one can walk or take a carriage. I suppose my brother has mentioned what we are trying to do to replace the Bow Street Runners, who while useful to a degree cannot carry the law far enough to prosecute and secure those who break the law with impunity. We hope to fill that gap and provide the community with some sort of protection and security. What sort of a community are you from, and are the laws that govern that community effective?'

Dick reflected before he spoke. He did not wish to sound superior while explaining how advanced society was in 1997 and that a community was largely law-abiding while facing stiff penalties for breaking the law. He began by explaining briefly how the system currently worked and that there was a large police force to monitor and apprehend criminals; that there were lawyers to defend or prosecute and judges and juries to determine the guilt or not of the accused.

John Fielding raised his eyebrows then frowned. 'I am afraid I do not understand. This is 1779. What do you mean by telling me that all this occurs in 1997? Are you a time traveller? A soothsayer? Please don't tell me you are a…witch?' He turned pale and reached for the arm of a chair, plopping down heavily into it.

'Not at all. I assure you I'm not a witch!' Dick laughed softly. 'I'm not a soothsayer either, or a fortune teller, but I guess I am a time traveller because I do come from the year 1997, where I am indeed a lawyer for those times and how I arrived here is a mystery I cannot explain. I wish I was a soothsayer. It could help.' His attempt at wry humour went over the heads of the brothers, who were swapping glances with each other and sighing.

Henry spoke first. 'Dick has explained this to me already, John. And I grant you it is indeed very fanciful and beyond any normal explanation but there it is. I am myself still trying to come to terms with his arrival and our chance meeting. Which,' he added,' could prove very fruitful in the end, given his wide knowledge of the law. Do you see, John, that with his help we could more easily organise a workable police system to protect our innocents! With advanced knowledge, we could have a huge advantage, could we not?' He took a breath, watching his brother for a reaction.

John finally spoke, deliberately and very slowly. 'My brother, I know you are not one to lie and whilst I find the story unbelievably fantastic in the true sense of the word, I have to suspend my disbelief. For now,' he added.

'I will help in any way I can,' offered Dick. 'While I'm not familiar with your laws, I will learn, and where I can offer helpful suggestions, I will. I may be here in your time forever or I may not, but it seems I have no control over it. And speaking of witches, I'm very ignorant about the subject as we don't have them in our time, er, my time. Only this morning, Mellie was telling me the most unfortunate tale of her mother and grandmother. Is it true that her grandmother was prosecuted and killed because she was considered a witch?'

The brothers exchanged looks.

'It is true. Mind you,' John added hastily, 'there are no witches abroad now but still some people who are ignorant and believe there are. I have heard that some women over in East Anglia, whilst proclaiming that they are simply healers, have been apprehended and tried in a people's court to be found guilty. One woman was old and because she had a cat, it was presumed that she must be guilty, as witches always had a familiar, the cat being the most common. Dreadful business. It is strange, but it seems that they have been, almost always, women.'

Dick paled. It was a terrible thing to even think.

'Oh, there have been terrible times closer to home, but in an earlier time around the late 1650s. I recall hearing about a Witchfinder

General called Matthew Hopkins who came to seek out heretics and witches. It is said that he was paid handsomely for clearing towns of witches. He believed that a mole, wart or even a flea bite was a sign of the Devil and used a jabbing needle to see if these marks were sensitive to pain. Apparently he rounded up nineteen witches in the one day. A lucrative business and he stirred up much superstition, to his advantage of course.' John paused, reflectively. 'You know, it's not that long ago, really. Makes me pale with disgust. And the torture the unfortunate women were forced to endure…' He stopped.

'Torture?' queried Dick. 'You mean they were tortured before being, er, executed?'

'My word indeed,' interrupted Henry. 'Everyone knows the history. Thumbscrews called pilnie-winks were used and iron caspie claws, which were a sort of leg iron heated in a brazier and clamped to their legs. I have heard that in between 1484 and 1750 some 200,000 witches were tortured, burnt or hanged in the whole of Western Europe.' He shuddered. 'At least we don't do that any more – well, at least not that I know of.'

'Well,' said Dick, 'back where I come from, a person can be called a witch but it's only meant to be derogatory and insulting, which is bad enough. Some old women who have hairy lips or moles attract attention and derision, which is cruel but harks back I guess to what you've been talking about. We like to think that we have advanced to a point where we treat our fellow humans with respect and dignity. But it would appear that we do not.'

'Quite.' John rang a little bell. 'I think we need something a little stronger than a cup of tea. Port for everyone? And then with some fortification in our victuals we may begin discussing our new and improved police force to come.' He attempted a laugh. 'At least we don't have to deal with witches any more. I hope. And Henry, do you remember not so long ago, that despicable character who used to stick pins in women as they went about their business?'

'Oh yes, I certainly do. Now, what was his name? Let me think.'

Henry stroked his chin. 'Rynwick Williams. Yes, that was it. I believe he received six years in prison. They used to call him the London Monster.' He laughed. 'You can see, Dick, how urgent our mission is, can't you?

Dick smiled weakly. For the first time since his arrival, he felt comfortable. Being able to offer his advice to the brothers Fielding gave him a sense of fitting in and being accepted as a Londoner. He was very grateful he had fallen on a softer inclusion than might otherwise have been offered elsewhere. What if he had landed, as it were, in a thieving environment, or in the middle of a hostile community who mistrusted strangers?

He had had many puzzled looks over the last several days and wondered why, as he was dressed to the best of his knowledge in the attire of the time. Anyway, for the time being he could prove useful. But his advice could only be of the broadest lest he should unwittingly change the course of history. Witches, men who stuck pins in women, what next?

Thus pondering, he strode along the narrow streets, dancing lightly across the uneven surface of the cobblestones and wondering how many backs had been broken in the making of this roadway. He was also struck by the number of taverns, far outnumbering any other commercial establishment, and stopping outside one of them aptly and proudly displaying its name Cobble Inn, decided to investigate.

He ducked just in time to avoid hitting his head on the overhead lintel and once his eyes had adjusted to the smoky haze inside, looked for a place to sit. The small windows offered very little light and would make it difficult to identify anyone. But Dick didn't know anybody, so that problem didn't arise. The clientele appeared to be mainly working class and he wondered why they were here at this early hour. But there was a purpose to their meeting which he was soon to discover.

He ordered a pint of their best ale and now accustomed to the gloom noticed about ten men huddled around a long hewn table, nursing their own ales, puffing on their long pipes and in deep discussion. It was hushed at first then a voice of dissension rose above the rest followed by a copycat reaction to what had been mooted.

Dick listened intently, leaning back into the gloom so as to not attract attention.

'Well, I seen her with me own eyes, I did. Long hair but blondish, not black as ye would expect. And no cat neither but I swear on me bairn's grave it was one of 'em. She had a wild look in her green eyes as if she'd never been around here before and her clothes were ill kempt.'

'Go on with ye,' a chuckle from one of the members. 'Look who's talkin'. Would you be a well dressed man about town yourself in those mangy clothes of yours?'

More laughter, this time from everyone.

'Why, you look like something yon cat's dragged in.'

The tavern cat did indeed look the worse for wear as it sat perched on the corner of the bartender's slab, obviously well regarded and not thought to be an accoutrement of any witch. It sat, its slitty eyes taking in the surroundings haughtily aware of its status, smug in its inscrutability as it preened its mangy fur.

'Well, I seen no witches around these parts. Never been as far as I know since the time of me granddad! Been on too much ale, I think, me lad!'

Another member added to the mounting hilarity. And yet, beneath this jocular little group, a certain uneasiness hovered. Dick could feel it and he was a complete stranger. Was this why they had congregated, to discuss whether or not witches still lived in their community?

'Come to think of it,' ventured a small mousy man at the far end of the table, 'I remember last winter when my old lady took ill. My sister brought a woman to see her and although I never spoke to her, I thought she was a bit, well, you know, not like us.'

'What do you mean, not like us?' asked another.

'I saw her mixing up a sort of potion. She had put a collection of little bottles of I know not what on the little table near my wife's bed. Took them straight from a bag that was hidden beneath her cloak, she must have done. They sort of appeared sudden like and I did wonder then…' He broke off, not sure where his argument was going.

'Well, did your wife recover or not?' A bullish man with ginger chin whiskers spoke up.

'Well, that's the strangest thing. An apothecary had been to visit her the day before but said there was nothing he could do and we prepared for her demise. But this complete stranger, known only to my sister, made up a potion and within a day and one night, my wife began to recover, the colour returning to her pale cheeks, the light beginning to return to her eyes. Now if that isn't the work of a witch, I'd like to know what else it could have been!' His little eyes darted around the group of men as he waited for a response.

'Has anyone else something to say on this matter?' The tall man, who seemed in charge of the proceedings, spoke quietly.

There were murmurings as the men muttered between themselves, reluctant to offer anything else in case they might appear foolish.

'Speak up, if you have anything to say. 'Tis not the time to be shy if a problem is occurring in our town. We must take action if there is a witch among us. I for one am not ready for the devil to take my soul. What about the rest of you?'

A large man raised his hand. He stammered a little as he spoke. 'Well, I myself haa…ddd a strange experience. It was me mother, d'ye see. She was ailing fast and the apothecary, like my friend here just said, could do nothing. I do…do suspect that the same woman came to my house too, unbidden by myself, you understand, but it would appear that me mother had known of her whereabouts and had begged for her to come. Well, she was me mother, wasn't she, and I wasn't going to say I wouldn't help, now was I? Well, she did get better. It was like like a miracle.' He stopped speaking abruptly.

'More like demon magic,' another muttered.

'Enough!' thundered the spokesperson. 'We need some ideas now. Can anyone who has experienced the appearance of our so-called, for the moment, witch, pen us a likeness? We can then attach it somewhere in the town square where all can see.' He waited while murmurings rose and fell.

'It has been said I have a fair hand for copying likeness,' spoke up a man who until now had been silent. 'I have seen her. She came to my brother's house not two moons ago. My memory has stored this image so I shall never forget. I could have a try.'

'Do it and we will meet back here in one week. Now, it is back to our chores afore the day gets much longer. I myself have many horses to shoe before the day is done.'

The meeting adjourned, the members filed out of the tavern, leaving Dick to ponder about the overheard conversations. Now just where would witches come under the law of his time? But he would mention to the brothers Fielding the uneasiness that apparently was bubbling away amongst members of the London community. If they had heard anything, they had not mentioned their disquiet to him. Perhaps it was not regarded as a problem to be handled by lawful investigation. He drained the remains of his ale and left the dingy atmosphere of the Cobble Inn.

12

Chloe hailed Lily, who showed her relief that help was at hand.

'Oh, miss, I could hardly believe how busy I was becoming. So glad you've turned up.' And it was true that Lily did look exhausted. How hard it was for her.

'Why don't you relax a bit on that chair and have some tea? I'll handle the customers for a while. Hang on while I go over to that stall and get you a mug.' She checked her pocket, hoping there would be enough. In fact, she had enough for two mugs and carried them carefully back to Lily's stall. Grateful hands reached up for the warming liquid.

'Thank you kindly. There's some that would not treat me as kindly as you.'

'Oh?' Chloe looked questioningly at Lily.

'You know, me whose husband has run off. Folks see it as my fault.'

Nothing new there, thought Chloe as she reflected on her own recent events. Whatever had happened to her back then, now was her journey and she must make the best of it. Lily was making the best of her journey and if they were to help each other out, then that was a good thing. For now.

Pippin looked like a coal monkey by the end of the day when Chloe stopped at the smithy to collect him.

Harry was happily snoozing and came to life as Pippin stroked him and untethered him for their return to the camp. 'He's been a busy lad, has young Pippin here,' said the blacksmith. 'I was late to start this morning, so things got a bit behind. But he is a plucky lad, I have to say, and he works well under direction. I admit I would have been worse off had he not been here this day. Off home now, are ye?'

'Yes. I think I shall have to throw young Pippin here into the river to clean him!' She gave him a friendly pat on the head. 'Now let's get going afore it's too dark.'

Dusk had almost given way to night as the weary workers pushed through the gate into the Gypsy camp. Small fires dotted about glowed and everyone was busy preparing for the evening meal. Perhaps it was their only meal of the day. Chloe felt blessed that she was able to buy some meagre provisions at the market thanks to the pittance she had received as her wages for the day. Others were not so well off, she knew.

Pippin tethered Harry beneath the now familiar oak tree. Someone had mysteriously left a small bundle of hay. There was also a small amount of firewood just beside the dead embers of the fire from the night before. Chloe looked around for her benefactor but no one was even looking in their direction.

A small fire was soon blazing and two tin mugs resting on the stones soon heated the water for the tea Chloe had been able to purchase at the market. The hard rye bread wasn't so bad dunked in the tea and, with victuals warming their stomachs, the two weary travellers were soon able to snuggle under the brightly coloured Gypsy rug and sleep.

At the first stirrings of dawn, the camp began to come alive. Fire embers were poked to entice new flames to warm bodies and to heat water for tea.

Fierce's wagon was closed. Her horse was nowhere in sight. Chloe wondered where she was and if she had returned during the night at all. But Fierce didn't take anyone into her confidence, it appeared. She remained distant even with her fellow campers and was aloof with Chloe and Pippin.

Rousing Pippin, Chloe wandered down to the stream to splash her face and wash briefly. The water was icy and took her breath away but she felt refreshed afterwards. Her dress was torn in several places. Lily had offered to help her repair it but as soon as one portion was mended, it ripped in another. It would soon disintegrate while on her, she feared. Perhaps with her new-found employment it might be possible to find another sturdier dress at the market, and the thought cheered her as she returned to hurry Pippin.

Fierce was tired and she was cross. It had been such a wasted journey across country to source some different, stronger reeds for her halters. She had heard that a small river some leagues from the camp grew wild and resilient reeds and rode most of the night to find them. By daybreak, she had found the river all right but there were no reeds in sight. Flare was tired too and they returned to the camp in a much slower mode.

The camp was deserted. The workers had long departed for their various occupations and her new tenants were also gone. She tethered Flare close to the river, where he might quench his thirst, throwing down some hay for his breakfast. She noticed something flapping on the door of her wagon and as she got closer saw it was a rough piece of paper attached to the wooden door with a small but sharp pointed knife! She caught her breath as she ripped the notice off the door, turning to see if anyone might be watching. Once inside, she sat down on her bed and opened the missive.

We know what you are. You will be found out and you will be given what you deserve.

The message was in rough language. It was not explicit but she quickly guessed the meaning and from time to time had received notes like this even though her mother was long gone, dying for crimes she never committed, for simply helping others to wellness.

It was strongly suggested that Fierce had the same tainted and evil gifts and she was aware of certain members of the community who held such views. She kept well away from the townsfolk. She didn't mix with anyone except her own kind in the camp but wondered just how long they would be able to stay if feelings ran too high and too many folk were afraid of them and wanted them gone.

Her hand shook a little as she quickly crushed the crude note in her hand and threw it on the floor. For the first time since her mother's death, Fierce felt the familiar feeling of vulnerability sweep over her. At a time long gone, she had feelings for a man not of her tribe. Their love was passionate, shared with an intensity Fierce had never known before. In her soul she had known, as had he, that it was a very special alliance. She remembered his touch now as if it were yesterday, his tenderness, his energy merging with her own and the feeling that seeps into the entire body when two souls connect. Now, try as she might, she couldn't remember his face; only his burning energy that sustained her for the time they were together. Then, one morning on waking, he had gone. No goodbye, no explanation, no warning. How her heart ached knowing he would never return, how she mourned her loss and how she cried for the missing of a love that was denied to her in the cruellest of ways. She was inconsolable for the longest time and now… well, now it was only in times of uncertainty that the painful memory sank its sharp point into her heart.

But this was no time for self-pity. She had work to do and, tired though she was, it was now time to fetch Flare. She shouldered the completed halters and in no time, rider and horse were streaking along the road towards the market.

It was a fine day, although a brisk wind eddied around the ankles of the skirted women and threatened to whisk caps of the menfolk's heads. Chloe was already at Lily's stall and Fierce nodded in her direction as she passed. She had no time for chit-chat, and what would she talk to Chloe about anyway? She wasn't of her kind and wouldn't understand the Gypsy way of life. For now, she would tolerate Chloe's presence. There was something she couldn't put her finger on in the way Chloe carried herself and how she was kind in her dealings with young Pippin to whom she owed nothing as he wasn't even kin.

Fierce often reminisced about her childhood, the happy times at the camp in Wales, the summer evenings sitting outside under a favourite tree listening to tales of generations long gone. And the music; the fiddle playing plaintively on the summer air, the lilting voices accompanying it. And then, just as she would be adjusting to a new camp, they would be on the move again. That was fun too for a young girl who had no inkling of the suspicions aroused in places they visited. Her mother would warn her not to mix with them in the towns, so she didn't. As she grew older and learned more of the Gypsy ways and traditions, grown-up talk would settle on her shoulders like a cosy shawl. She learned that her family name, Ingram, had been taken from a local (non-Gypsy) resident in the hope that it would help protect them against racial attack. It made her fearful and she had no wish to fraternise with townspeople. She was also aware that some Gypsies were guilty of stealing sheep, horses and of committing other felonies and that they earned their living by trickery or by telling fortunes. But she also knew that most Gypsies lived by a strict moral code and many were followers of the Christian faith.

Farmers who knew the Gypsies were quite content to have them stay in their fields and would share the fruit from their trees, the vegetables from their garden. They looked forward to their return each season, when they would help by working the land. In the villages at the local inn at eventide, merry dancing would be accompanied by the harp and fiddle.

Those were peaceful times but Fierce was too young to remember and would lap up the stories at her mother's knee. Now, she was weaving her own story that would one day become a part of the Gypsy history, or herstory, and she would smile at this. Never in the past had a woman been the leader of a Gypsy group, even one as small as hers. How times had changed.

As she was arranging her halters on the hewn table, a few interested folk stopped to admire, touch and even ask questions about the durability. Occasionally, she would sell one and, if lucky, two.

'Only the finest reeds are used for these halters. I make them myself and they are much more comfortable for the horse than conventional, hard leather ones. You will find it so.' She would not push but gently persuade and often her tactic worked well.

On this particular morning, a gentleman of obvious wealth and position stopped, fingered one of the halters and held it up. 'And how much, my pretty, are you asking for this?' he asked.

'Half a crown, sir.'

'For something that comes from the weeds in a muddy river? Surely you jest?'

'I can assure you, sir, that my halters are made with excellent and clean reeds that grow on the banks of a virgin stream,' Fierce replied proudly.

'And where did you spring from? I can tell you are of Gypsy blood and the colour rising in your cheeks as we speak must mean you have a fiery disposition. I dare say you have done your share of stealing and profiteering, eh?'

Fierce was aware that he was baiting her but she kept a cool head, even if her cheeks didn't look cool. 'I come from an honest family, sir, and have never stolen anything in my life.' She took a deep breath and added, 'But you, sir, are the one attempting to steal my reputation away from me. Now, if you are interested in purchasing a bridle, you are most welcome. If not, then please stand aside to allow others to approach!' She knew she was tempting fate but she would not let him sully her family name.

'You are an insolent wench. Someone should take to you with a whip. No doubt you have a husband who would willingly do so if you spoke to him as you have spoken to me!' With a look that would sizzle the grass, he turned on his aristocratic heel and marched off.

Fierce swallowed and was glad to see him leave. How she would have liked to peer into her crystal ball to see what would become of him. She hoped there would be no repercussions but her next customer showed no rancour and in fact bought two of her halters. She sighed with relief, knowing that this night she would indeed feast with perhaps a draught of wine to warm her cockles.

That evening as Fierce was counting her earnings for the day, voices shouting disturbed her. She threw open her door and standing at the top of her steps saw some men jostling each other, arguing loudly.

'They are not of us,' one shouted angrily. 'They cannot stay here. It is bad luck.'

'We don't know anything about them,' complained another. 'They could rob and kill us for all we know.'

Fierce stepped down quickly and marched over to them. 'Keep your peace!' She spoke authoritatively. 'Chloe and Pippin are kind, gentle folk. No, they are not of our kind but will not endanger us. Where is your compassion? You were not raised to be so judgemental. Now leave them be.'

Their mistress had spoken. The little group broke up amidst mutterings of discontent.

Chloe and Pippin stood well back near their tree.

Fierce strode over to them. 'Don't you mind what you have heard. They are restless, that is all. Times are hard and when their tempers are raised, newcomers make them feel threatened. It is nothing and soon they will come to see that you are no threat to them.'

This was the first time Chloe had seen Fierce smile. 'It's all right,' she smiled back. 'We understand. I can't tell you much more about us than you already know. Soon we will be able to move on and we are thankful you are allowing us to stay here.'

'Hear, hear,' added Pippin, grinning. He was beginning to enjoy his young life and if this was how Gypsies lived, then he wanted to be one too. All that mattered to him was Harry, a few coins to feed them both and a place to rest in the evenings. If travelling was a way of life, then he would embrace it.

13

Fierce sat on her bed. The crumpled note that had been attached crudely to her door sat there, mocking her. She picked it up and read it again. Who would want to hurt them? They never caused any trouble. She could foresee a time not too far into the distance when they would indeed have to move on. She also pondered on the threatening behaviour of the gentleman who came by her stall earlier in the day. Well, the note had been put on her door long before she had seen him. But who, then?

She could feel the frown forming like a storm brewing. She had been raised to be strong, to stand up for herself. Her brothers, stocky twins moulded in the image of her surly father, treated her like another brother but there was never a place for tears or fears. She kept the fear she had of her father hidden as best she could. She knew that her Da's consequences were harsh and random depending upon the level of his intoxication or his mood. Fierce defied him once. Her back still bore the scars from his heavy leather belt. She learned to hold her tongue, a tongue not made for silence, a character not built for reticence.

The love and tenderness she received from her Ma hovered with a low but resistant flame encircling her heart. It would come from within Fierce when an intended recipient showed the intention to nurture and respect it. Her own quickness to anger would rise at the very whiff of an injustice, but it did not come from a bitter spirit.

She had watched her mother over the years bravely withstand the constant insults and physical beatings from a husband whose anger, once released, would strike the fear of any God into a recipient or into one who watched. And Fierce was witness to her mother's irrevocable decline, finally falling victim to her detractors who put her to death. She was laid out on the little white bed in their cottage, a hand-woven blanket covering her violated body. Fierce knelt and held her mother's thin, lifeless hand. Her grief was deep and cutting. Her father knelt on the other side of the bed almost bent in two as he leaned into his wife, shoulders shaking, his usually harsh voice reduced to a childish whimpering.

Fierce brushed the tears from her eyes, willed the sorrow to leave her heart. Her mother had long gone to her rest. Her father too, but she wondered if he was at rest; truly at rest. She was making the best of the gifts bestowed upon her. No use labouring over the ills of the past. The present was more than enough to contend with. Sooner or later, the identity of the one who had left this crude note on her door would be revealed. It was only a matter of time and Fierce was a patient person, only acting when the time was right.

Dick mentioned what he had witnessed in the tavern to the Fielding brothers.

'Hmm, most interesting. I didn't think the feelings were as strong. Obviously these folk still believe that witches live amongst us. That is plainly ridiculous, if you ask me. But, well, it will be very illuminating to see whether this poster stirs up more ill feelings? When did you say they are meeting again, Dick?' Henry looked at Dick over his glasses.

'Next week. I guess they will put up a poster, or several, about town. Then we can see just what a witch looks like, can't we?' He chuckled.

A week had passed with urgent discussions between Henry, John and Dick. They were of course very interested in Dick's experience and he was only too willing to share it. It was obvious that some sort of law and order was vital to make the town a safer place.

'Let me tell you, Dick,' offered John, 'what our dealings with the law are and how they operate now. With your permission, of course.'

'Certainly,' replied Dick. 'I'm new here and I'm interested in how things are done. If, and only if I can offer any assistance, I shall be only too pleased.'

'Good man. Now where shall I start?' John stroked his chin and began. 'Policing is so much better than it was in the, er, old days, eh, Henry?' He winked at his brother.

'My word, yes. Do go on,' Henry chuckled.

'We used to rely on private individuals and part-time officials – that is, many victims of crime were able to identify and apprehend the culprits before contacting a constable or a justice of the peace to secure their arrest. Witnesses were legally obliged to apprehend those responsible for the crime and to notify a constable if they heard that a crime had been committed. Now of course, this individual responsibility has been eroded and replaced by constables who now do the apprehending of anyone accused of a felony, do you see, Dick?'

'Yes, I understand,' replied Dick.

'We do have night watchmen on the streets between about ten at night and sunrise to examine suspicious circumstances, and during the day, city marshals and beadles. Of course, Henry and I (not that we wish to brag, of course) had set up a practice of hiring thief-takers on a retainer who, when a crime was reported, were sent out by the magistrates to detect and apprehend the culprit. These were the Bow Street Runners and I must say that they made a comfortable living out of it and soon we introduced other innovations such as collecting and disseminating information about crimes and suspected criminals, making the Bow Street office the centre of a criminal intelligence network. It has been working quite well and more offices have been set up since. As a result, many offenders now appear at the Old Bailey, which has been operational now since, um, 1673, a little before our time, eh, Henry?'

'Quite,' acceded Henry with a smile.

'And, it can only get better,' continued John. 'Oh, and there's a state prison just nearing completion. That should take a load off the small police stations. And here's where you might contribute, Dick. We need a sort of central Act to mobilise a police force to maintain constant watch and see that the law is observed. What do you think?'

'Well,' said Dick slowly, knowing full well that Robert Peel's

Metropolitan Police Act came into being in 1829 under the control of the Home Secretary. 'I think you may be on the right track there. I am only a lawyer but it seems to me that the police force should be uniformed to create a presence.'

Nods from the brothers Fielding.

'Moreover,' continued Dick, 'as a result of frequently patrolled streets on prescribed beats, the opportunities for crimes to be committed would be reduced significantly, wouldn't you agree?'

'In principle. In principle,' nodded John slowly. 'I understand your inference. This would mean that a greater weight would be placed on the prevention of crime! Capital. Capital!'

'Well, that's all I have to say on the matter,' sighed Dick. 'I think this is more suited to your capabilities than mine.'

He could have continued to say that Millbank prison would turn out to be a disaster and be denounced largely because of its substandard drainage that caused many deaths through contamination. It would be replaced by Pentonville prison in 1842, but the brothers did not need to know that. Not now. All would come to pass much later than their time.

'Dick, how can we thank you for your ideas? Novel, I must say, but indeed worthy of consideration. I think this calls for a little celebration. Port, I think?' John Fielding opened the crystal cabinet, drew out three glasses and the now familiar bottle of ruby port.

Taking a small stroll in the early evening before supper, Dick stopped dead in his tracks, confronted by a poster with a likeness that was so familiar, he felt himself pale.

Wanted. For suspected witchery. Reward Forty Pounds.

The penned likeness was of a youngish woman with long, dark blonde hair and a frank expression. The colour of her eyes could not be detected, but were given the impression of a pale regard. They could have been blue.

Dick felt his heart beat a little faster. Why did this image look so familiar? He couldn't recall meeting many women, if any for that matter, since he had been here in London Town. He was perplexed and after standing in front of the poster for some minutes, walked on, his mind in turmoil. He came across another of the images on a wall in the next street and the further he walked, the more he found. He began to recall snippets of conversation amongst the men he had seen in the Cobble Inn that day. Was this the witch they had mentioned in not too pleasant terms? He shivered, felt like tearing the poster down, but did not want to attract attention. He wasn't a Londoner.

Mellie's excellent stew graced the table. She dished out a sizeable portion for each of the men and withdrew to the kitchen.

'You say you saw the witch?' enquired John.

'Well, not exactly. I saw the likeness which had been penned and attached to several places around the town. It is a very artistic and realistic portrait of a woman and it's strange but I feel I know her. Yet that's impossible. I know no one here of that description.' Dick frowned.

'I can see it is of some consternation to you,' spoke Henry softly. 'Perhaps it is a face you have seen in your travels. It happens like that sometimes and we feel we have known them from somewhere. It could be as simple as that.'

'You're right. I'm sure you're right, and I can't explain why it bothers me.' Dick poked at his stew.

'I know what you need, lad. You need the company of a good woman! That's what ails you, my man! You will come with us when we enjoy the hospitality of Mrs Justice Montgomery. She is holding a function to raise money for a children's orphanage. We will introduce you as our distant cousin. Say you'll come.' Henry patted Dick's arm.

'Well, I don't know. I'm not good at socialising and…'

'Now is the time to start getting better at it,' John interrupted. 'It's settled, then. This Saturday night. Oh, and don't worry about attire. We can help there.' He winked at his brother and took a long draught of his wine.

14

'Chloe, whatever is the matter?' Pippin turned to see her standing in front of a large tree beside the track. 'Come on, we'll be late!'

Chloe didn't hear and was transfixed by the small poster nailed to the tree trunk. It was indeed just a penned likeness but it was a likeness of her! It was the same likeness she had discovered earlier on their travels on another tree! She still had it in her pocket. She then read the words beneath the image and felt immediately faint. *This cannot be! There is a mistake, for sure.*

'Chloe, come. What are you looking at?' Pippin went back to where she was standing and saw. 'Oh, my duck's feathers!' he uttered. 'Why, that's you, Chloe! But, but you're not a…a…a witch. Are you? Are you?' he repeated as his eyes flicked from her face to the poster and back again.

'Of course I'm not! How could you even suspect such a thing?'

'No, but…well, I don't, but how could that poster be up there, then?'

'Somebody's made a terrible mistake. Someone who has guessed that I'm not from these parts and wants to cause trouble. Oh, Pippin, we shall have to be extra careful now! It's most important that I find some different clothes to wear afore I'm recognised. This is an awful state of affairs. I've heard what they do to witches but I didn't think that still happened now. I mean, this is civilised London Town. People aren't superstitious like they used to be, are they?'

'There's some that are, I'm afraid, Chloe. And there will always be some troublemakers, mark my words. Can you ask Lily if she has some clothes you could borrow? Now, quick, wouldn't do to linger too long here now.'

Lily's face broke into a huge smile when she saw Chloe. 'For a minute, I thought you weren't coming, but I'm glad you're here again. Why, whatever is the matter? You look terrible.'

'Well, I've just realised how terrible I do look in these tatters. I have nothing else and I'm hoping you might be able to help me out? Anything would be better than this.' Chloe pointed to her worn-out skirt.

'I'll have a look tonight. Mind you, clothes are not plentiful in my house but we are about the same size. I could loan one of mine to you. Can you wait until tomorrow?'

'Yes, and thank you. I would be very grateful. Now, let's see how well we can do today.' Chloe wrapped a piece of cloth around her to serve as an apron and waited for customers.

Pippin was late finishing at the blacksmith's and she was glad that night had almost come as they made their way back to Fierce's camp. Her fear of detection was mounting and the safety of the Gypsy clan would be welcome. Harry had not come with them as he had been limping after his long journey over the past weeks. He nickered his welcome as the duo passed through the farm gate. Pippin ran to him. The smithy had given him a few carrots; pure gold for a horse like Harry.

Chloe poked at the embers, knelt down to fan them as the little fire valiantly stirred further and began to flame. She was startled by a voice.

'It's only me,' Fierce said, squatting down beside Chloe. 'Don't be nervous. But I can understand if you are. I saw your poster in the town.'

'But it's not me,' protested Chloe. 'I'm not a witch! Yes, I'm a stranger in these parts but I am not a witch! You don't believe I am, do you?'

'I know you are not,' replied Fierce firmly. 'I can spot a witch a league away. But I know what it means to be labelled. It has happened to me too and only just the other day.' She explained the incident that had occurred at her market stall.

'What can we do? I've heard terrible tales but I thought everything was in the past now.'

'Yes, the terrible witch hunts are a thing of the past, mostly,' Fierce sighed.

'What do you mean, mostly? No one really believes the stories any more, do they?'

'Well, Chloe, unfortunately there are always those who want to stir up trouble. Unhappy folk who want to see another punished. My mother was cruelly hunted down and killed for being a witch. She was a healer and helped many people with illnesses but because she did that and folk were superstitious and ignorant, she was branded. My own father didn't lift a finger to help her. He was a hard man.' Fierce paused and closed her eyes as if she was remembering. 'When he was angry with me, sometimes it was because he was drunk and he would yell and hit me until I brought him another ale. I was too afeared to refuse. But he used to beat me when he wasn't drunk as well. My Ma used to chide me, "You are a fierce little 'un." After that, she called me Fierce all the time and the name stuck. She knew I hated my father when he was violent but all she said was that it was his way. She never said a bad word about him. I am proud of my mother and her service to humanity when all other methods to heal had failed. She was much ahead of her time. And now…' she trailed off.

'Now?' Chloe prompted.

'Well, now I fear for my own life because there are those who will believe that I have inherited the traits of a witch!'

'Do you have some of her healing ways too?' asked Chloe.

'Yes. And her potions. Some I have made myself using the ways of nature, where lie all the answers if one knows where to look. Even my braided halters are made from river reeds and are as strong as nature herself. But seriously, Chloe, you need to be careful about what you say and do. Your likeness is abroad now, so someone has seen you and deduced, wrongly of course, that you must be a witch because of the way you look and because you are a stranger to these parts. Folks here are very suspicious of strangers, as I found myself when we first took up our camp in this field. A lot of folk are also superstitious and nothing will shake a belief once it has rooted.' She didn't mention the note that had been nailed to the door of her wagon the previous night and had made her aware more than ever of her vulnerability.

'Lily has promised to loan me one of her dresses, with a bit of luck,' said Chloe nervously.

'We will have to do better than that. We will change the colour of your hair for a start.' Fierce shrugged off her own problem.

'What? How will you do that? You don't have any hairdressers here.'

'Well, that is a word I do not know, but remember, I am expert in dying the reeds all manner of colours for my horse halters. It will not be difficult. Now, let's see what colour would be the most suitable.' She ran some strands of Chloe's hair through her long fingers. 'Black will be too dark because your skin is very fair. I think a pale chestnut colour would do very well. Come to my wagon this night when Pippin is sleeping and we will get to work. Now I must prepare for my evening meal.' She smiled confidently and walked quickly back to her wagon.

Chloe nibbled at her bread and drank but half her mug of tea. Her appetite had been whittled away by fear and she was glad of the anonymity of darkness softened only by the glowing dots of camp fires. Harry was hanging his head and no doubt already in the land of nod. Pippin was snoring and, covering him more closely with the Gypsy blanket, Chloe stole quickly over to Fierce's wagon. She tapped on the coloured door.

'Chloe! Is that really you?' Lily was startled at the new person behind her stall.

'Yes, it's me. Didn't you recognise me straight away?'

'No, I certainly didn't. But the new colour suits you. If I had seen you walking in the street, though, I would have never known it was you!'

Chloe was pleased with this last comment. More pleased than Lily could know.

'I've brought you this.' Lily opened a paper parcel to reveal a dark brown dress with several buttons down the front. 'It's not much but it's all I have. I hope it will do,' she smiled anxiously.

'It's just perfect!' Chloe held it up. 'What do you think?'

'I think it was made for you and it goes so well with your new hair.' She giggled. 'Don't forget to take it with you tonight.'

Pippin was non-committal on seeing Chloe's new hair. 'It's OK, I guess. Just doesn't look like you, though, that's all.'

'Good! It's very good. The whole idea is to not look like me!'

'I suppose so.' He walked silently all the way back to the camp.

'Pippin, you start the fire. I'm just going over to Fierce's van for a minute.' Chloe had noticed that Flare was tethered near the stream, so knew his mistress was home.

'Chloe!' Fierce flung open the door. 'Come in. Come in. I'm preparing some vegetables for supper. What's in the package? A present for me?' she joked.

'Well, no, it's a different dress and I wanted to ask if I could change into it here, in the privacy of your van.'

Chloe changed behind the floral curtain. The dress fitted her very well and when she stepped out, it was with Fierce's complimentary remarks.

'A well fitting dress in all ways,' she commented. 'My, all those buttons! No one will know you. Well, that is what we hope. Now, would you sup with me? There's plenty for Pippin too if you wish.'

'I shall not refuse your generous offer, as I'm starving! I shall fetch Pippin. Thank you!' Chloe felt her face flushing as she stepped quickly down and hurried over to where Pippin was tending Harry. She was unaware of the sidelong glances that came her way from several of the men sitting around their fires. She was unaware of the glances they exchanged between themselves.

'Pippin, we're going out to tea! Now, down to the stream with you and wash off all that soot!'

'Tea? And where would that be? Is this another of your jests?'

'No, Pippin. Fierce has asked us to her wagon. We,re having vegetables! Can you believe that? I,m hungry just thinking about it. Now, off with you.'

Fierce flung open her door. 'Come in, come in...' she began and noticed the note pinned to the wagon door. Another one! She blanched, pulling the note off quickly and ushering her guests into the warm and inviting wagon.

'Are you all right?' asked Chloe, noticing Fierce's ashen face. 'Postman left you a letter, I see,' she joked.

'I am perfectly all right, thank you. Postmen don't visit Gypsy camps and it's none of your business,' she snapped.

'Oh, I'm sorry, I didn't mean to pry. Just joking...' she added lamely.

'Don't,' retorted Fierce. 'We will have our supper now. Sit.'

The two guests sat. They ate. Fierce remained silent. Chloe kept her eyes down, feeling very uncomfortable. Whatever that note said had really upset her hostess.

'Well, that was a lovely meal. We had better be going now. Thank you, Fierce.'

Chloe held out her hand. Fierce didn't take it.

'Good night, Chloe. Pippin.' Fierce all but pushed them out the door.

She sank to her knees beside the bed and read the note written in the same, spindly uneducated hand as the first one.

Start your magic – but it won't help you. these will be your last days Liza. We are coming for you.

Fierce felt her throat close over slightly. 'Ma,' she whispered. 'Ma, help me. Who knows my name? Why do they persecute me? I have done nothing wrong. Tell me what I should do.'

The lilting tune of a Gypsy folk song drifted through the open window. Soft voices were singing, but tonight Fierce did not feel like joining them. Many were not happy with strangers in their midst and she thought it best to keep to herself this once. Through the open window, she could hear strains of a very old Irish folk song. Although not a particularly typical Gypsy tune, it was one her mother used to play on an old harp but hearing it on a fiddle did not spoil its haunting melody and Fierce felt the tears coming as she remembered.

Aderyn Du
Blackbird with silken wings
And golden beak and silver tongue
Will you go for me to Cydweli,
To ask how my love is?
One, two, three things are difficult for me:
Counting the stars when it is freezing
Placing my hand so that I can touch the moon,
And understanding the mind of my loved one.

15

Dick preened just a little as he stood in front of the mirror. He had never been to a governor's residence, not even in his time way back in 1997. It would be a new experience. If only he had his camera – but that wouldn't be invented for another forty-six years. He would just have to commit the image and the experiences to memory to take back with him. But what if he could never return to a life that seemed so normal and predictable and so…familiar? Perhaps this was, after all, just a very good dream; a very, very good dream indeed. Whatever it was, he was loath to wake up just yet. Things were beginning to become interesting.

The coach arrived at the precise time of seven-thirty to take the brothers Fielding and their newly found friend, Dick, to Mrs Montgomery's fund-raising event.

The sweeping driveway of immense proportions was an awesome sight, even for someone of the twentieth century to behold. Dick was impressed by the well laid-out gardens, much like he had seen in *House and Garden* documentaries, but he had never visited one that wasn't just for tourists.

Daylight was beginning to fade and huge candelabra were already lit in readiness for the guests so they could make their way safely inside. It was very romantic. Dick was now remembering his own exposure to history, in particular the inventions of Alessandro Volta, an Italian physicist who invented the electrical battery. He went on to discover methane electricity but that did not come into its own until the late eighteenth century. So households, even mansions, lit their way with candles. The poor could seldom afford candles so made their own with rush sticks and hoarded fat, or they dipped the rushes in fat and put them in metal holders to make rush lights. Not here. The

Montgomerys were not poor and the candles blazed in a vast display of light. Dick would not be broadcasting his knowledge of the invention of electricity, as it would probably be seen as fantasy.

Lady Montgomery, married to Lord Justice Montgomery, was a woman of most ample proportions. She stood imposingly at the top of the grand stone staircase, her upswept hair arrangement complimented with many strings of pearls (probably authentic, guessed Dick) hanging from her large neck and dangling down onto her very matronly bosom.

Her preferred colour appeared to be royal blue and her gown matched the curtains, the carpets and even the livery of the servants, who looked like characters from a period play. Except that this was real; it was not a home merely frequented by curious tourists. Lady Montgomery ushered them into a large, reception room where a motley group of guests were already assembled.

The Fielding brothers introduced their cousin to her and she expressed her delight at meeting such a charming young man. Dick found himself blushing, the ruffles around his neck itching more vigorously, and he wished he'd not come. On one side of the room was an enormous buffet table, easily twenty feet long. It simply groaned with delicate dishes of the day from canapés to bowls of exotic food, aspic meats, plates of roasted poultry and some dishes Dick couldn't recognise.

In the centre sat a huge bowl of what looked like party punch, surrounded by small cups with little handles. He wondered if it was laced with some alcohol and hoped it was, as he was dying for a drink of something fortifying. Apparently, so were the brothers, as they guided him towards the laden table. There was definitely alcohol in the bowl and Dick could feel himself relaxing.

People were milling about and he smiled and bowed as if he belonged in this environment, and they smiled back assuming he was. There was much chatter. The ladies fluttered their fans. The room resounded with rich male laughter.

On the far side of the room, he noticed a woman, standing on her own, remarkable for her stunning emerald green robe and diamante tiara. She caught his regard and smiled before lowering her lashes. He turned around, looking for John, who was nowhere to be seen. When he cast a look across the room again, the woman had disappeared. He tried to be inconspicuous as he moved about the room, hoping for another glimpse of the mystery woman. In his imagination, the image reminded him of Chloe. He didn't see her again.

The assembly was called to attention by Mrs Montgomery, tapping a spoon gently on a crystal glass. There was an immediate response and within seconds the room was hushed.

She spoke at some length about the reason for the gathering, imploring everyone to dig deep into their pockets as the function was specifically to raise money for an intended orphanage to house disadvantaged children. Much clapping followed, murmurings and back-slapping as decisions were made on amounts to be donated.

Dick hoped he wasn't going to be conspicuous as the only one who wasn't going to donate. He slipped out through the tall glass doors onto a terrace which fortunately was not too well lit. He felt like a thief skulking in the bushes but he breathed in the welcome night air, grateful for this escape route. The sky was clear. Myriads of bright stars graced the heavens and a gentle zephyr brushed his cheeks gently. Who would know he had been thrust into an unfamiliar period of time? He would have seen the same stars back home and, for a moment, felt at peace.

'Well, what did you think of Mrs M?' John Fielding asked Dick as they relaxed back into their seats of the carriage for their homeward journey.

'What? Oh,' Dick brought his attention back to the present question. 'Oh, she seemed pleasant enough. She does seem dedicated to helping the kids. So that's good.'

'Kids?' John looked perplexed.

'Oh, an expression that means children. Very common where I, er, come from.'

'Indeed. Most unusual. Yes, she is a delightful lady. I hope everyone was supportive. She is in agreement with me about the urgency of the plight of street children.' He turned towards Dick. 'Not that you were expected to contribute, my dear boy. But who knows? In time, you might be earning a great deal and then, well, we'll see, won't we?' His eyes twinkled. 'I must say I am feeling rather fatigued. Must have been that delicious concoction we were drinking.'

'Punch,' said Dick.

'Excuse me? Did you say punch?' He laughed. 'Well, we've got one on you, my boy. I didn't think you would know about it. It's been around for a long time. Of course you know that it was invented as a beer alternative years ago by men working the ships for the British East India Company. About 1655, I think, it became popular in a general sense, wouldn't you say, Henry?'

Henry nodded and added an extra comment. 'I doubt whether it should have been as strong as the beverage we imbibed this evening. Not that I'm complaining,' he chortled.

'Well, I didn't know that, I have to admit,' Dick said. 'Good stuff, though. And you're right about the alcohol, Henry. I could hardly walk out the door.' He turned towards John. 'Er, John, there was a very attractive woman at the gathering. You must have seen her. In an emerald green gown, with a tiara?'

'No, I can't say that I did. But there were quite a few people there. I see your romantic side has not died, eh? Did you speak to her?'

'No, I turned away for a moment and when I looked again she had vanished. Completely vanished into thin air! Are you sure you don't know her? I think I have had too much to drink. Imagining things now.'

'I must say I didn't see anyone of that description. Did you, Henry?'

Henry was leaning back into his seat, fast asleep and snoring contentedly.

'Oh well, thank you for taking me. It was very, er, very enjoyable. When is the old girl having another party?' Dick asked.

John had joined his brother in sleep.

16

Chloe had settled in nicely at the stall of her new friend, Lily. They worked well together and more money was beginning to change hands. Chloe had a way with customers and could sell. Further up the row was Fierce. She had been busier than usual. The braided halters were selling well this week and even her readings had taken an upturn. It seemed that the ladies weren't about to take much notice of their disapproving husbands. They wanted to know what was in their futures. Fierce had an uncanny way of tapping into the truth of things. She was very intuitive and detected undercurrents that most folk were unaware of. She never made up anything just to satisfy the customer. If she didn't pick up anything, she would say so, which was disappointing but better than lying. Honour was very important to Fierce.

Just as Chloe was finishing a small transaction, she heard the sound of raised voices that seemed to be coming from Fierce's stall. And indeed she heard correctly. She craned her neck and saw a couple of well-dressed 'gentlemen' leering across at Fierce in a most threatening manner.

'Hold on, Lily, I'll be back in a minute. I think my friend is in a bit of trouble.'

By the time Chloe had walked the short distance to Fierce's stall, the voices were becoming louder. Fierce was defending herself and her voice was strong too. She wouldn't back down to anyone. Except this time when one of the men leaned in very close, holding his fist within inches of her face.

'See this, girlie? Well, this will land squarely on your pretty face. You're a menace to a God-fearing community, peddling your pagan wares. And as for that, that crystal ball over there,' he gestured, 'well, that's just pure evil, it is. My good lady is getting notions, she is, and I will not have it. Now, you stop your nonsense or I'll have the constabulary onto you. Do you understand? Do you?' He thrust his red face even closer, shook his fist and walked off.

His friend echoed the threat. 'Yes, you destructive wench. You should be under lock and key. And we'll make sure you are if you don't stop this nonsense!'

'Fierce! Are you all right?' Chloe asked anxiously when she felt it safe to approach the stall.

'Yes, why wouldn't I be?' she replied defensively. 'A couple of ignorant and rude men. You wouldn't expect them to behave any better, now would you?' Her face had paled in spite of her casual attitude and her hands shook slightly.

'No, I expect you're right. Still, they could do some damage. Perhaps they have influence with the authorities too.'

'Well, I'm not doing anything wrong. People come here of their own free will. I don't force them.'

'Yes, they do, but you know that most of the wives are heavily influenced by their husbands who control them and want to continue doing so. They're not going to take kindly to anyone who encourages freedom of will, or choice for that matter. One day things will change, but for the moment, you had better be careful. Perhaps the crystal ball should be, um, locked up for a spell.'

As soon as she had said this, Chloe realised she had made a pun but Fierce had not noticed, fortunately.

'I'll think about it. I have nothing to fear. The readings are very popular, you know. I need to make a living.' She frowned. 'Well, you had better return to Lily. I'll see you later at the camp.' She turned away.

By the time Chloe had returned to the Gypsy camp, the skies were darkening.

Pip was almost invisible so black with soot was he, but he grinned through the dirt and seemed happy enough. 'I'm learning how to be a smithy,' he said proudly. 'One day I might have my own business.'

'That you might, too,' smiled Chloe. 'Now down to the stream with you and get cleaned up.'

She cast a look in the direction of Fierce's van but there was no sign of movement nor was Flare grazing anywhere in the field. Feeling concerned, she decided to walk over to the van. She scribbled a note and was just about to slip into the crack between the door and the archway, when she noticed a note already rudely attached with a large nail to the door.

She looked about her. The camp folk were going about their evening chores and she could see no sign of anyone that might not be welcome. Feeling a little as if she was prying, which of course she was, she read the note, in a very bad hand and practically illegible.

YOU HAVE BEENE WORNED. YOU WILL BERN LIKE THE UTHER WITCHES!

Chloe gasped. This was dreadful! Poor Fierce. What would she do? What could she do? Chloe ran back to the oak tree, where Pippin was sitting leaning against the old trunk.

'What's the matter with you?' he asked. 'You look like you've seen a ghost!' he chortled.

'Not exactly, but I did see something that wasn't very nice. Someone left a nasty note for Fierce and I think she might be in some sort of trouble.'

'What sort of trouble?' What's she done?'

'She hasn't done anything. It's just that…it's just that, well, I don't know if I should say…'

'Come on, say it, Chloe. We're partners, aren't we, you and I?'

Chloe drew in a breath. 'Some folk are saying that Fierce is a witch. Now, you mustn't say anything about this. To anyone, do you hear? And especially not anyone at the markets.' Chloe looked stern.

'I promise I won't. She's not, is she? A witch, I mean?'

'Of course she's not. Nor more than I am a witch,' but even as she said it, Chloe remembered the poster with her own likeness nailed to a tree. Someone thought she was a witch. Ridiculous! Well, back where she had come from, absolutely ridiculous. Here, she was not so sure.

'What should we do?' Pippin looked anxious.

'For the time being, nothing. Fierce hasn't even seen the note yet. She's not back. There were a couple of men at the market who threatened her this afternoon. I do hope nothing has happened.'

As she spoke, Flare came thundering into the field. Fierce tethered him quickly near the stream and strode purposefully towards her van. Chloe saw her stop short as she saw the note on the door then disappear quickly inside. Chloe's note had gone unnoticed. She would wait a little while then go over to see if she could help.

<h1 style="text-align:center">17</h1>

Dick's introduction to London society had been interesting but he wasn't all that anxious to repeat the experience. He was interested in helping the Fielding brothers. He paused and chuckled to himself as it sounded as if they ran a circus. He could see the need for more law and order particularly as the town was growing and would continue to do so. He was also interested in following up the story about the poster with the strangely familiar girl's face upon it. Henry suggested they go to the Duck's Inn and keep their eyes open for anything that might throw some light on the puzzle. Some chance in there, Dick thought. It was so dark you couldn't see your own hand in front of your face. But go they did.

The poster was also stuck on the wall just outside the tavern.

Henry paused to study it before entering. 'Pretty thing,' he mused. 'Hard to say why anyone would think she was a witch, though. She looks far too nice. So you think you know her, then?'

'Henry! That's her!'

'Her?'

'The woman I saw at the Montgomery house! The woman you said you didn't notice.'

'You must be mistaken, Dick, my boy. This woman on the poster is obviously from a lower class. Now, how could she undergo a miraculous transformation enough to be invited to Mrs M's function and look, as you said she looked, most agreeable? I think you have had a touch of the sun.'

'No, I haven't!' Dick felt a little insulted. 'If they're not one and the same, then just what is going on here?'

'I apologise. I could perhaps enquire, next time I see Mrs M, just who the mystery lady was. Would that help? If it is connected to your previous life, then it is none of my business really. We all have pasts that have been, shall we say, not always to our liking or of our making. I am sure the mystery will clear up one way or another. Now, let's go in, shall we?'

While the brothers sipped their ale, Dick wondered about the prevailing attitude towards witches and the dreadful practices committed against these women accused of witchcraft. Ghastly, archaic and cruel, to say the least. *Doesn't happen in my world. We have laws to stop things like that.* The more he thought about the woman at the benefit at the Mongomery house, the more he began to doubt himself. It was possible his imagination was playing tricks but what if it wasn't?'

'We're glad you're here, Dick. For the moment, this is your world, Dick, and although I don't think for a moment that these practices take place any more, there are those who would like to see them restored. And,' Henry added for good measure, 'some are powerful identities who should know better. They create fear and then find a reason to justify what they have created. It's a nasty business.'

'Yes, I know, and I will contribute as much as I can to help you get some laws up and running. As soon as possible. Another pint, Henry?'

'Yes, why not? Let's just sit quietly and watch what might happen. We could get lucky.' He grinned.

Almost as soon as he had spoken and just as he was about to lift his pint to his lips, the tavern door burst open and three fellows tumbled in. They ordered pints and selected a table near a grimy window. They began talking to and over each other. It was impossible not to catch most of their rather illiterate conversation. Dick and Henry sat back into the gloom and were silent, sipping and listening.

'Not on my watch. There's some around, I'm telling ye. We might have been told that no more of these evil creatures are roaming the land, but they are. Why, only the other day I saw one with my very own eyes.'

'Go on, and where might that have been?'

'It was early, barely light, and I was outside my house having a bit of a…well, you know…when I saw this strange woman coming out of a house across the way. She was carrying a basket and she wore one of them cloak things with a hood and all. She was looking about as if she didn't want anyone to see her.'

'That don't make her a witch. My wife sometimes wears a cloak. And she's no witch. Well, only in the bedroom and that's good!' He laughed raucously and the others joined in.

'Here, take a good look at this. I nicked it off the tree in the square. This wench here is wanted for being a witch.' He held it up to the light.

Dick couldn't help seeing it and recognised it as being the same one he had seen. He caught his breath and nudged Henry. 'That's the same likeness,' he whispered. 'Now what do we do?'

'Nothing. We just listen and we wait. Any information could be useful. Another pint, Dick? We might as well be comfortable, lad. We could be here for a while.'

In the latter part of the afternoon, the next day, Chloe noticed that Lily was not her usual self. She was pale, looked tired and had trouble concentrating. By five o'clock, she almost seemed on the point of collapse.

'Lily, you must go home. You aren't well, I can see, and you should be home resting.'

'I cannot. There would be no rest at home anyway. I will be all right. I'll just sit for a bit.' Sit she did, but by five-thirty, she wasn't any better.

'You stay still now, Lily. I'll just run up to the smithy and tell Pippin I'll be back at the field a little later and for him to go on alone. Promise me you won't move?' Chloe placed a caring hand on Lily's shoulder.

'All right. I will wait until you come back.' She managed a very weak smile.

Pippin was not totally in agreement that Chloe should return on her own later.

But she was adamant. 'I can't leave her like that, Pippin. She is most unwell. I will be fine, I promise you, and I should be back well before dark. Now don't you worry. I shall see you later, all right?'

Pippin shrugged. He saw no good reason why he should argue with her any longer.

'Oh, Lily. You are certainly not right. Come on. We shall close now and I'm taking you home whether you like it or not.'

Lily was in no position to argue. She knew she was ill.

The walk to Lily's house was longer than Chloe had expected, and by the time they arrived, Lily was almost ready to collapse. The cottage, in very bad repair, was deserted. Her husband was obviously not back from wherever he had gone. Chloe sat Lily down on one of the chairs and, investigating the little kitchen, found a pitcher of water and poured a cup for Lily. There was no fire going, so Chloe found just enough twigs and dry leaves to start one. But how? There were no matches here or anywhere around for that matter. Had they even been invented?

'Lily, how can I get a fire started so I can make you a cup of tea?'

'Oh, Chloe, there's a tinderbox over there in the corner but it is difficult to manage. You will find a piece of touchpaper up there on the mantel. Next to it there should be a piece of flint which, when struck on the back of a knife, should produce a spark to light the paper.'

Chloe felt for the paper, found it and the flint. After many attempts and much sweating, she succeeded in producing a spark onto the touchpaper, which she blew on gently until there was a flame. She quickly placed it onto the mound of dry wood and leaves under the grate. It smoked at first then, miraculously, flames began to shoot up and started devouring the fuel.

Lifting the heavy kettle onto the grate, Chloe stood back, wiped her forehead with the back of her hand and turned to Lily. 'Well, that was some challenge. How do you manage to cook like this all the time?'

'Not too difficult when you know how – it's all we know, isn't it?' Lily replied tiredly.

She was grateful for the tea and drank it thirstily. Chloe helped her to her bed and almost as soon as she lay down, her eyes closed and she was sleeping soundly. Chloe felt her forehead and she didn't seem to have a temperature, so she covered her gently with a thin blanket lying in a heap at the foot of the bed and left the cottage. Here was one depressed woman, the loss of her children weighing still heavily on her heart and would be forever more, no doubt.

No wonder Lily was tired. She worked at the markets and tried to keep her home clean but it was obvious that it had become too much for her. The small windowpanes were too grimy to even let light in. The excuse for a kitchen had a very large hearth that hadn't been swept in many a week and the sleeping area was dank. It would be fair to guess that the husband was not very fussy about personal hygiene. Getting in between the couple would be a dangerous thing, so supporting Lily from a distance was the only option for now.

Chloe passed the market stalls, all closed up now. Everyone had returned to their homes for the evening. Darkness was beginning to descend casting unfamiliar shadows across her path. She quickened her walk, feeling weary and missing the comforting companionship of Pippin and Harry. She fancied she heard a footfall behind her and turned quickly but saw nothing. It could have been a rabbit. But she heard it again, swivelled and thought she caught a glimpse of a human form, but it vanished before she could identify it.

Fear sat on her shoulders now as she quickened her step even more. She knew now that it wasn't her imagination. Turning again, this time she made out two figures approaching her, not making any attempt to disguise their presence. She started to run but before she could get very far, a heavy hand grabbed her arm, twisted it and forced her down to the ground. As she looked up to identify her assailant, a fist made its mark on the side of her head and her attempted scream was swallowed up by the darkness of unconsciousness.

18

Back at the field, Pippin was becoming concerned. It was now fully dark, the camp fires being the only source of light. He ran over to Fierce's van and knocked timidly on her door. When she opened the door, she saw immediately the worried look on his face.

'Miss, pardon the intrusion, but Miss Chloe has not returned yet. Miss Lily was poorly, and she took her home and told me to go on. So I did. She should have been back by now, don't you think?'

'Pippin, you come with me. We'll go back and see if we can find her. Quickly now.'

The two raced over to Flare. Fierce leaped onto his back, reached down and swung Pippin on behind her. In seconds, they were away through the gate and galloping along the narrow track towards the markets.

Pippin cast his eyes from side to side, hoping to see Chloe. The track was deserted. He clung more tightly to Fierce, who had now slowed Flare down. Suddenly, she stopped him. She slid down off her steed and ran to the side of the track.

Pippin followed. 'What is it? What do you see?' He very soon saw for himself Chloe's crumpled body in the shadow of the hedgerow.

Fierce bent down, feeling for a pulse. 'She's alive. Pippin! Hold Flare still while I lift Chloe up onto him. We must hurry back before it is too late.'

Flare's strong body carried the threesome back to the Gypsy camp. Fierce dismounted quickly and slid Chloe off and into her arms. She carried her quickly to the caravan.

'Fetch me some clean water, Pippin, from the stream. Hurry now.'

Pippin did as he was bidden as Fierce laid Chloe down gently on her bed. She was pale and her breath was coming in short stabs. She had bruises on both her arms and on her head. It was a miracle she was still alive. Fierce reached for her healing box on the shelf above the bed and took out some medicaments, examining them for an appropriate one. She firstly placed a few drops of arnica into Chloe's mouth for the shock, then gently began dabbing some arnica tincture on her bruises.

By the time Pippin had returned with the water, a little colour was beginning to return to Chloe's cheeks. Fierce made a hot cup of chamomile flower tea and, supporting Chloe, persuaded her to sip it slowly.

When at last Chloe opened her eyes, she struggled and began to scream.

'Ssh! Chloe, dear. It's all right now. You are safe.' Fierce stroked her cheek.'

'But they were going to kill me. I couldn't run fast enough. I tripped. They…'

'They? More than one? Oh, you poor girl.' It was then she noticed a piece of paper pinned to Chloe's skirt. She gasped. It was the likeness of her. Chloe had been given a terrible warning.

'Chloe,' Fierce spoke gently. 'You must rest now. You will stay here with me this night and you will be safe. Tomorrow we will talk about all this and what we can do.' She encouraged Chloe to sip a little more of the tea. 'I will be just outside. It is a beautiful night, very still with the scent of jasmine in the air. Can you smell it? Not much of a moon but that makes it easier for all of us to sleep peacefully.' She looked down at Chloe, who was slowly drifting off to sleep. She looked up at Pippin, who had all the while been standing at a respectful distance, obviously concerned about his travelling companion.

'Will she be all right, Miss?' he asked in a small voice. 'Did they try to kill her because they thought she was a witch?'

'What do you know of such things?' retorted Fierce angrily.

'Not much,' replied Pippin softly, not wanting to inflame the situation. He would keep his mouth shut until such time as Chloe gave him permission to open it again.

'Well, whatever you might have heard, or seen, you know nothing, do you hear me? If Chloe is in danger, the less you say or see, the better. Do you understand?' Fierce stared intently at the sooty youth standing in front of her. There was no doubt as to his loyalty to Chloe, but this attack was foreboding and the less he knew the better off they all would be. 'Now, be off and get some sleep if you plan to go to work tomorrow.' She gestured towards the door.

'Yes, ma'am. I will. Good night, Chloe,' he whispered in the direction of the sleeping woman.

Fierce took a warm blanket outside and put it on the lee side of the van. She doubted she would get much sleep. As she lay there looking up at the skies and the stars that held so much beauty compared to some of the ugly things that happened on earth, she tried to come to terms with the evil abroad. Both she and Chloe had received warnings now and while it was not new to Fierce, it was nonetheless still very disturbing and frightening. She could only imagine how it must be affecting Chloe. Perhaps it was time to hold a meeting with her fellow Gypsies and take them into her confidence. She was going to need more support than a sooty boy and his ancient nag.

19

Henry sipped his ale slowly, leaning back in the anonymous darkness of the booth he was sharing with Dick. If they had any more ale, they would both fall asleep. He sat up straight with a start. His excellent hearing had picked up something and he listened intently. He laid a hand on Dick's arm and raised a finger to his lips.

'And there she was, brazen as you like, at the markets mind you; in one of them stalls. She was sellin' some cloth and there was another slip of a girl with her. I tell you, it is the same one as the likeness we been puttin' about the town. The exact same. Hair a different colour but the face and those eyes – those pale eyes like nothin' I ever seen afore. Well, Alf and meself followed her after the markets be closed. At first she went back to the cottage where the other girl lived then walked back past the markets. It was just getting dark and she didn't notice at first that we was followin'. But then she turned round and Alf wasn't quick enough to hide so we decided to grab her there and then. Gave her a good walloping as a warnin', we did, and left a callin' card. We stuck one of them poster things to 'er dress. She'll get the meaning when she wakes. She'll learn that we want none of her sort in these here parts.' He grunted with satisfaction, waiting for praise from his listeners.

'Maybe ye killed her,' said one.

'Maybe ye knocked her brains so hard she won't remember why you did it,' said another.

'She was still breathin' when we left. Honest,' counteracted the storyteller.

'Where was she goin', then? She could have been goin' to a whole nest of witches for all you know.'

'Well, we walked along a bit and afore long, came to a large field with lots of little campfires. There was wagons. A Gypsy camp, I'm guessin'. Now, it don't take too many brains to know that them Gypsies spawn witches, mark my words.'

'Well, did you have a look?'

'It was dark. Who knows how many of them and only two of us. Why tempt fate. We did our bit. We did enough to send a clear message.'

Henry and Dick exchanged horrified looks. A potential powder keg was about to go off.

'We have to do something, Dick. Can't let innocent women be knocked around like that on a suspicion.'

'What do you mean? Are you saying that it might be confirmed on investigation that she is a witch?'

'No, no, no. Not at all. A figure of speech.'

'Not a figure I like particularly,' replied Dick.

'No, well, what I plan to do is visit this camp and see for myself. Yes, that would be a good idea.'

'If you don't mind a suggestion, Henry, might it not be better if I went? I'm unknown in these parts and a little more able to defend myself, if you'll pardon the inference. You are known to represent the law, such as it is, and that might deter the inhabitants of the camp from talking. If you see my meaning.' Dick withheld a small smile.

'Umm, I do see your point, dear fellow. Perhaps you are right. But what if they set upon you, then where will you be?'

'I'll be running my legs off as I escape.' Dick laughed. 'Don't worry. I have a black belt in karate and know how to defend myself.'

'And pray just what is a black belt?' Henry was puzzled.

'A special award in the martial arts. An oriental method of defence and very powerful when learned correctly.'

'I see I have a lot to learn about your ways, my dear boy. Can you show me this special defence one day?'

'I'd be delighted, Henry.' Dick stifled a chuckle. 'Now, let's make a bit of a plan. You will of course be my back-up – my second, if you prefer to put it that way. No, I'm not going to be shot but you might need, just might need, to run for some constabulary help.' Dick grinned at the perplexed look on Henry's face. 'Now, I think we'll talk further when we get back, and the walk will sober us up too.'

They walked out, not daring to cast a backward glance at the little group of witch hunters who were now doing some serious drinking, voices rising, tongues getting looser.

Dick's horse riding skills were minimal. He had taken a few lessons at his wife's behest but didn't see the point in a suburban environment. But now, well, he visited the local blacksmith to enquire just where he could find a pleasant-natured, mature, understanding little horse that wouldn't throw him off.

'Ah, sir, I know of just the right one for you. New around here are ye?' the smithy asked.

'Visiting. Just visiting and thought a casual little trot up a country lane might be amusing.'

'Well, if you'll just come behind here, I'll show ye.'

Dick followed and sure enough a quiet little mare, chestnut, was chomping on some hay in her little enclosure. She looked just the right size for Dick.

'Looks perfect. I shall only want to ride for a couple of hours. How much do you charge?'

'It will be half a crown, sir.' He smiled genially.

Dick felt it was a fair transaction, watched the horse being saddled and in gingerly fashion put one foot in the stirrup.

'Other side ,sir,' suggested the smithy.

'Of course. You're right.' Dick changed to the left side. 'Um, do you think you could give me a hoist up? It's been a long time.'

The smithy obliged and once Dick was firmly in the saddle and had adjusted the stirrups to the length of his legs, he felt more or less comfortable. He felt some of the lessons coming back to him as he nudged the flank of the mare and urged her towards the gate the smithy opened for him.

'Good luck, sir. See you in a bit. If you go up that lane yonder, it is a pleasant journey. You'll come across a Gypsy camp but don't you worry about them. They is gentle folk and you won't come to no harm.' He doffed his cap and waved Dick off.

Walking the horse until he got his equine bearings, Dick wriggled to feel his seat more securely. The mare didn't need too much urging. She was obviously used to being ridden and within about twenty minutes, Dick was feeling quite at home and began to enjoy his rural surroundings. He thought the smithy had looked familiar but couldn't place him.

Then his mind wandered back to his previous life. He remembered he had a wife, back then, back in a time that was becoming increasingly distant in his memory. Would she be worried? Were they happy together? Unanswered questions surged through his mind, yet he was surprised that he was not missing any of his other 'life'. He had adapted so well to his life here in London. It was like a holiday, really, not too taxing but interesting and challenging. He was meeting new people. His skills were sought after and he relished being taken seriously. He was enjoying his life for the first time since, well, a long time ago.

'Well, old girl,' he spoke to the mare, 'I think you've been along here before. I don't even have to drive.' He chuckled to himself, noticing that they were approaching a large field with lots of oak trees. This would have to be the camp.

'Whoa, girl. Stop!' And she did, right opposite the gate.

Dick looked in and could see half a dozen vans. A few campers were doing chores and he supposed they were the Gypsies in question. He noticed a very large and magnificent-looking black horse tethered near one of the vans.

Suddenly the door flung open and a tall, dark-haired woman appeared. She looked in his direction, stepped down and, patting the horse, untethered him and walked towards the gate.

'Did you want something?' she asked Dick in not too friendly a manner, tossing her hair back as she spoke, revealing a large golden earring.

'I'm looking for someone and I wonder if you might be able to help me.' He pulled out a crumpled poster of the wanted girl and showed it to Fierce.

'No one like that here,' she said, handing it back to Dick. 'Why do you want to know?'

'Well, I saw this poster in the village and thought the face familiar. It might be someone I know.'

'And it might not be someone you know.' Fierce pulled on Flare's halter as he tried to get closer to the gate to smell the mare. 'We don't have strangers here, so I can't help you. I have to be leaving now so if you would kindly back up your horse so I can get out…'

Dick obliged, watched her swing effortlessly up on to the massive black horse and, with very little urging, head him off in the direction of the village. He sat quietly for a moment, thinking. Then, not wanting to waste any of his enjoyment, continued up the lane a little further. But he hadn't come to sightsee and he quickly turned his mount around, stopping once more at the gate.

A woman was sitting on the steps of one of the other caravans, enjoying the sun. Dick decided to take a chance. He tethered his little mare, opened the gate and walked over to the van.

Chloe was startled, still feeling fragile from the other day. She stood up quickly, shading her eyes from the strong morning sun behind the stranger coming towards her.

'Excuse me,' said Dick. 'Please don't be alarmed, but I just want to ask…' Then he stopped dead in his tracks. This was the face of the woman on the poster. She was pale with light blue eyes and longish hair that was a cross between blonde and auburn. She was dressed in a simple peasant dress. Once again, only more strongly this time, he felt he knew this face, but from where?

'Yes, what do you want? Strangers are not welcome here. You had better leave before the camp leader returns.'

'That was the camp leader? The woman with that magnificent black horse?' Dick asked.

'Yes.'

'Do I know you?' Dick asked. 'You look very familiar. Could we have met somewhere recently? I can't imagine where, as I haven't been here long.' He stared at her until he realised it must seem rude.

'Well, I don't know you. Perhaps you've seen me at the markets. I work there.'

It was Chloe's turn now to be confused. She wasn't going to say, but she too felt he had a familiar face. She hadn't met many men other than those who came by at the market, so she had no idea where they might have crossed paths. She began to feel a bit dizzy. Her head had not settled since the beating. She began to sway and Dick lunged quickly and caught her just as she was about to fall off the step.

'I'm sorry but I was attacked the other night and I'm not quite right yet.'

'Attacked! Where?'

'In the lane on the way home.'

'So it was you! I heard some fellows bragging about it in the tavern. This is terrible. We have to stop these things happening.'

'Well, I don't know how you can do that, single-handed. It's nothing to do with you. Now you must go before Fierce comes back or things will be unpleasant.' She stared at Dick intently. There was a look in his eyes that disarmed her; a familiar regard that she couldn't place. 'I'm Chloe,' she almost whispered. 'Now please go. I'm all right and you don't know me. We've never met. Goodbye. And thanks,' she added, 'for catching me right now.'

20

Dick swung himself off the horse. His legs felt like jelly and it took a while for his gait to become normal.

'Did ye find your journey pleasant?'enquired the blacksmith searchingly.

'I did, thank you. Perhaps I'll do it again. Soon,' he added smiling. 'Good day.'

Dick didn't mention his little adventure to Henry right away. He wanted to think about the girl and to try and solve a puzzle. Because a puzzle it was. He was not in the habit of forgetting people, their faces or experiences. Being a lawyer, it was necessary for him to have a keen and retentive memory for details.

The girl's face was beginning to haunt him. He also felt afraid for her. She could be attacked again and had no protection except her friends at the Gypsy camp. And that camp leader. She was an unfriendly sort.

That night, Dick slept fitfully, tossing and dreaming. He dreamed he was in another time; a time of unhappiness, a time when he had felt his life was taking a turn for the unknown. He reached out to grasp a hand that was close by but the hand withdrew and disappeared.

Just at that point, Dick woke up, sweating. His heart was thumping and he thought deeply about the dream before it could vanish and the meaning be lost. Yes! He remembered a time when he was depressed and unhappy, when his sanity was at stake, when he felt he just had to get away from…from what? That was the burning question. Was he running from someone? Was he being chased? Nothing came to him. All this must have happened before he left 1997. Just what did he leave behind?

A face flashed before his eyes. A face that he had seen recently. It was the face of the Gypsy girl he'd seen that day. It was the face of the girl who had been attacked. She was very pale for a Gypsy, he thought, and there was no reason why she should slip into his consciousness. He was not dreaming now. The image wasn't fading and made his questions seem all the more urgent. Did she remind him of someone he had known in a previous life? Was that someone the reason he had found himself here in 1779? He felt on the brink of a discovery, an illumination, a lead towards some explanation, and then it slipped away with the image and he was left again wondering and questioning.

'So you had a visitor, I'm told,' said Fierce, an edge to her voice. Obviously she had not deterred the stranger from entering the property. '

'Yes. At first I was frightened but he was a kind gentleman.' Chloe would not have to bring up the subject after all. 'He said be knew my face but, in truth, I don't know him. He was genuinely attentive and concerned about my plight. You've never seen him before?' Cbloe asked.

'No, he hasn't been through the markets while I've been there. I suppose he has also seen the likeness of you as others have and somehow thinks he may know you. Chloe, I have to ask you and I've never done so before out of politeness and because you're a guest in my camp, but,' Fierce paused, choosing her words carefully, 'how came you to be in these parts?'

'Well, you know I came with Pippin and Harry. We just happened to stop here without any plan at all.'

'No, I mean before that. Before you met Pippin. I know he isn't your nephew.'

'No,' Chloe lowered eyes. 'He isn't. We saved each other by joining forces, if you like, travelling the road. When I saw that poster, I was so frightened. How can someone put a likeness of me out that in public when they've never met me? I don't understand. But Fierce, I'm not meaning to deceive you. I just didn't know how to explain my presence. I remember enough to know that one minute I was at a meeting in 1997. I collapsed and knew nothing more until I woke up dressed in country garments – in a field in 1779, I found out later. I couldn't understand why no one would help me. Everyone I met along the way ran away from me, calling me vile names. I even got thrown out of a tavern – bodily thrown out! It was so humiliating. If it hadn't been for Pippin, who himself had fallen on difficult times, I'd be dead I'm sure. It is a strange tale and no more strange to you than it is to me. I still feel as if I'm living a bad dream. So, I'm sorry to be a burden but I don't know what else to do.' Chloe had been holding back tears but now they came unbidden, streaming down her pale cheeks.

'Hush now, Chloe. You have been through a terrible time.' Fierce appeared unfazed by Chloe's story. 'I don't understand fully but I do believe you are telling the truth. If anyone else knew, they would suspect witchcraft. I don't want to worry you but you can see that, can't you? People just don't jump from one century to another. It seems like magic. You'd be judged a witch. It's bad enough for me just because occasionally I provide some healing herbs for those who are unwell and understand enough to seek my help. For the ignorant, that's enough proof to condemn me. It's been done many times before. My own mother died a cruel and horrible death because she was judged a witch for healing folk. What people don't understand, they will vilify. It happened many years ago, but there are still those who hold fear and suspicion in their hearts.' A hint of anger tinged her voice.

'And yet you've managed to survive, Fierce. You're respected and even if you have been shunned by some ignorant folk, generally you are respected, aren't you?' Chloe felt the tremor in her voice.

'As long as I don't mingle too much with other folk and mind my own business, yes. Even here in the camp, there are those who would wish me gone. Many of the men don't like a woman in charge. Oh, they accept it a little unwillingly but do so because I'm seen as a strong leader and I believe I am. I treat them well and I've earned their respect. But the winds of change are always lurking in amongst the willows. Yes, I am strong but the strength has come from many hurts and sorrows. And you will have to be strong too, Chloe. I won't judge you for where you've been or where you decide to go in the future. But for now, we're here and together will be stronger if you stay.' Fierce chuckled. 'I never had a sister and I'd be honoured if you'll agree to be mine. We can have a small Gypsy ritual to symbolise it.' She smiled.

Chloe hesitated for a moment but she could see that it was an offer from the heart and she could also understand that it made sense to stand together against a force wanting to destroy them both. 'I'd like that, Fierce. I'm not sure just what my strengths were or are now, but I believe in fighting for the truth in one's soul. I'll return to the market tomorrow. I feel renewed and I'm concerned about Lily being there on her own.'

'You'll need to keep your wits about you. And don't ever again return here alone. You must promise me.' Fierce looked long and hard at her new sister.

'I promise.' Chloe smiled. 'Don't worry. With Pippin and Harry to protect me, I'll be fine.' She wanted to believe it would be so.

The next day, Dick reported his little adventure to Henry but all he could say was that the woman who had apparently been beaten up was alive and under the protection of the leader of the Gypsy camp.

'Extraordinary. Extraordinary,' said Henry. 'But we cannot be idle and do nothing. It might happen again to someone else. Once ignorant folk get a bee under the bonnet, there's no telling what can happen. And they can raise panic in a town, causing all sorts of trouble. No, my son, we have to act and quickly. We will organise a town meeting, appoint some honourable folk as marshals to keep watch on a situation that could easily become inflamed. What was done is against the law and these vagrants must be warned that an action like that cannot go unpunished.'

'It's all very well to say, Henry, and I do agree, but how are you going to enforce this?'

'I will write to the government. The Fieldings are not completely unknown in certain circles. This is a serious situation and could well finish up as a dire emergency.'

In fact, Henry directed his enquiry to none other than King George III himself. He was quietly surprised to receive a reply, not from the King, but from The Most Honourable Charles Watson-Wentworth, 2nd Marquess of Rockingham. Henry's enquiry had been met with the utmost sympathy and with the suggestion that the culprits who commit an offence on one person in the year of 1779 were indeed committing offences on the whole of society and should be brought to justice forthwith. Moreover, the justice system was to be used with full force, using the police, the courts and prisons systems.

Henry was delighted and he and John together drew up a list of offences punishable by law in the interests of crime prevention in the city of London, 1779. So now, the police force, provided with uniforms, would be set up with full authority to enforce the law, protect property and limit civil disorder. Their powers would include the legitimate use of force.

Dick would do all he could to help the brothers implement the setting up of the documentation. For him, it was like going back into history well and truly. He remembered during his own study of the English legal system, a quote by the English judge, Lord Coleridge JC:

> It would not be correct to say that every moral obligation involves a legal duty; but every legal duty is founded on a moral obligation.

But he knew that with the best intentions and the best legal system, many criminals would slip through the cracks. Nothing had changed from 1779 to Dick's own time in 1997. Right now, he was determined to protect a young woman from the evil clutches of witch-hungry, ignorant thugs, even if it meant getting personally involved. How he would manage was unclear; for now, he couldn't even think of a solution. He wasn't welcome at the Gypsy camp and he felt pretty sure that the leader would be taking a protective stance against one of her clan. Dick couldn't know that Chloe was just as much a stranger to these parts as he was.

Posters of a different kind were now appearing all over the village. Posters that had been designed and printed by Henry stating that any violence committed against a person or persons would lead to apprehension, trial and imprisonment, signed by the chief prosecutor. The Bow Street runners, red breasts and all, would soon be marching to a different tune.

Lily was already there when Chloe arrived, pleased that she didn't have to walk too far. Harry could, at a pinch, carry her but she worried about his old bones.

'Are you all right now, Lily?' Chloe asked.

'Right as rain, I am. Don't know what came over me, I truly don't.' She smiled at her new friend.

'Well, I do.' Chloe tied her apron on. 'You were just plain exhausted. I can come and help you with your household chores for a while if you like. And to check up on you to make sure you're eating properly.' She wagged a finger at Lily.

'Chloe, I'm all right. Really! I did miss a few meals and sometimes I can't sleep all that well. Rory snores something terrible and he is a bit of a hard taskmaster, I'm afraid. To tell the truth, I have to say that when he is away at the crofters doing the buying business, I am much relieved.' Lily laid out the materials on the stall table. 'But he's a good enough man and he doesn't beat me.'

'Well, I'm so pleased to hear that! I promise I'll leave you alone then. Now let's get started.'

Business was pleasantly brisk. By the time the sun was high in the sky, Chloe's tummy was beginning to rumble. She offered some of her bread and cheese to Lily.

'Oh no, I couldn't. Didn't have time to bring any lunch myself today but I couldn't take yours. Anyways, I'm not hungry.'

'Eat. That's an order.'

Chloe looked around the market as she nibbled on her bread. In the distance, she saw a figure she recognised and hoped he wasn't coming to their stall. But he was and, as Dick approached, Chloe began to feel a little nervous.

'Good morning, Chloe. I trust you are in better health than you were the other day.' He raised his hat.

'Thank you, yes.' She felt herself blushing as she felt his eyes settle upon her. 'Can I help you with anything?'

'Oh, no. I haven't come to shop. I came especially to seek you out and to make sure there have not been any other, er, incidents on the laneway home.'

'No incidents. But I will not be walking back alone any more. I have learned my lesson.'

Dick was about to reply when he felt a hand on his shoulder. He spun around. 'Henry! What are you doing here? Shopping for something?'

'No, my good fellow. I came looking for you and somehow I knew you would be here. Do you think it is wise to come?' Henry looked over his shoulder. 'There are bad feelings rising in the town and I wouldn't want you caught up in any, er, scuffles.'

'Scuffles?' repeated Dick. 'What do you mean? Henry, I would like to introduce my friend, Chloe.' He turned to her. 'Chloe, this is Mr Henry Fielding. Perhaps you have heard of him? He's helping to organise a proper police force to protect citizens like you and me.' He smiled.

Henry bowed slightly, took Chloe's hand and kissed it. 'I am most delighted to meet you, young lady. So you are the one who has been having a few problems lately.'

'Well, sir, only one, but it was bad enough. I hope you can catch the ones who attacked me. It was very frightening and I wouldn't like it to happen to anyone else around here.'

'We will be doing our best. You are not from these parts, are you? I suspect that the attack was just a prank against a stranger in town.' Henry tried to make light of it.

'Prank! I would not call it a prank. It was a deliberate attack on my person. And the language they used was vile and insulting.' A catch was in her voice as she continued. 'I am not a witch, as they called me. There are no witches any more. Anywhere,' she added for emphasis. 'I expect my incident to be taken seriously.'

'My dear, I can assure you that it is being taken seriously. Dick here is my partner in crime, as it were, and together we will hopefully bring about the cessation of such unwarranted attacks.' He smiled with some assurance. 'Well, it was enchanting meeting you, Chloe.' Henry doffed his hat, nodded to Dick and moved away.

'Do you really think this will happen?' Chloe addressed Dick.

'Chloe, please don't look so concerned. Henry is a man of his word and utterly reliable. He will leave no stone – no legal stone, that is – unturned in an effort to apprehend these thugs.'

'He does seem very nice. I'm sorry if I sounded rude.' Chloe blushed slightly.

'Understandable under the circumstances. And you weren't rude, just a little, um, forthright. And there's nothing wrong with that. In any century.'

Chloe gave him a very direct look. 'What do you mean, in any century? That's a very strange thing to say.' She had not mentioned how she came to be in London, let alone her method of transport, because she still wasn't sure how she had arrived. It wouldn't do to arouse suspicion at this time either.

'Oh, I didn't mean anything in particular. Just a manner of speech.' Dick now blushed a little. 'I'm also a stranger to these parts, that's all, and, well, it was only an innocent remark. Please don't be offended. Anyway, I have taken enough of your time. I shall leave now and perhaps our paths will cross again, who knows?' Dick bowed.

'Who indeed knows?' Chloe smiled rather stiffly as Dick touched his hat and moved away from the stall.

Her past was still a blank. Had she known him as a friend? Was he simply very like someone else she had known before? She wished she could remember more than the snippets she had shared with Fierce.

If she ever should meet him again, she would be very careful of what she divulged. Tongues wagged and ears listened, that she knew, and the only person who was privileged to have her own ear was Fierce. She could think of no reason why she would be at all interested in where this stranger came from. He wasn't in any danger and she felt it unlikely that he and his friend could help her with her plight. The Gypsy camp gave her all the protection she needed for the moment and, as for getting to and from the market, Pippin was her faithful escort, while Harry was like a fortress on legs.

21

Dick sat in front of the fire, a glass of Henry's excellent ruby port in his hand. He stared into the flames as if wishing for an answer to come about his circumstances and why he couldn't remember much about his past. He was deep in thought when Henry walked in, sat down opposite and began perusing a large folder with bulging papers.

'Well, m'boy. We are making progress, I have to report. The government is supporting us, the townspeople are supporting us and our new police force is now resplendent in very official and seemly uniforms fit for a growing metropolis. The law breakers had better watch out now.' He chuckled. 'Dick? Dick, are you asleep?' He leaned over and tapped his friend on the knee.

'Oh, Henry. I am sorry. I was rather deep in thought. Can you tell me again what you just said?'

He was enthusiastic about the law enforcement and congratulated Henry warmly.

'My dear Dick, you played a very large part in this. I will be forever grateful and so will John, I know. More port? And now tell me your troubles because they are bothering you in no small way, I can see.' He smiled encouragingly at Dick.

'I'm troubled not least because I don't know why I'm here and also because that girl I introduced you to, Chloe, seems so familiar, and yet I cannot for the life of me place her. She has a very feisty spirit and even that strikes a small memory chord but other than that I have no clues.'

'Well, all I can say is what I have said before. Answers may come or answers may not come. You must be patient and I am sure that there will be a satisfactory outcome. Just you wait and see.' Henry put a finger on the side of his nose.

Now just what did Henry mean, Dick pondered. Perhaps that

was all he could offer as he knew even less and was doing his best to comfort his friend. For the time being, Dick had no choice but to enjoy the company of Henry and the warming port. Would tomorrow take care of itself?

Chloe lay, awake and watchful. The clear skies above boasted a myriad of stars in an awesome celestial display. No other light save for a few dying embers from the fires in the camp. Pippin was sleeping soundly and even Harry was breathing deeply and probably asleep also. Chloe breathed deeply, filling her lungs with the warm night air. How pleasant it was to be sharing the night with nature and, despite her earlier experiences, how safe she felt. She could summon up the fear certainly, but also dispel it quickly. Perhaps it was partly because Fierce had made her feel secure. Fierce was not afraid of anything as far as Chloe could tell and here, in the little Gypsy fortress without walls, a calm reigned, cushioning any errant fears that might try to enter the consciousness of its dwellers.

Fierce also lay awake but she was thinking. She too was aware of the celestial display which could be seen from her caravan window and would normally lull her into a peaceful sleep but tonight she was alert and watchful. While she had played down the dramas that had been unfolding, she was wary and knew that more would come into play. How to protect Chloe was paramount. How to protect herself was a challenge she was ready to face as her proud ancestors had always faced. She could not stop the suspicions of ignorant minds any more than she could stop the stars twinkling. She was grateful that the newly formed police force might have some impact but the spurious underworld activities still holding onto the belief that witches continued to roam the lands worried Fierce intensely. Chloe had no idea of the real and present dangers that lurked in the town, in small country enclaves where tension was mounting towards a very unsettling degree that would lead to one intention only: to rid society of evil. That evil was the witch!

After many sleepless hours, Fierce had a plan. It was time to move her little band of Gypsies, and with much haste. They would travel north through country and wilderness. Fierce had no choice now but to trust her instincts, holding true as they had always been since birth. She would know when they reached safety. Her small tribe would not be happy to travel with an outsider but Chloe was now her adopted Gypsy sister and they would have to accept the decision of their leader. Fierce also was concerned that Chloe would not want to leave Pippin and Harry, but the old horse would not have the stamina to travel and besides, Pippin now had a good job with the trustworthy smithy. His future would be in his own hands.

Early the next morning, after breakfast, she summoned her tribe together to inform them of her decision to leave.

'But we are happy here,' spoke one.

'This is the best field we have camped in for many a while,' said another.

When Fierce explained the reason for leaving, there was loud dissent.

'This woman is not of our tribe. She is not our responsibility. She will bring bad luck,' chorused several.

Fierce remained centred. 'I understand your concern. I have been through many harsh times when, accused of being a witch, I have found it impossible to defend my honour. There are parts of our land where Gypsies are accepted, perhaps more so than around these parts. I also have a duty towards my adopted sister to protect her. She is not able to defend herself. She is no more a witch than I and I know that, as you have loyally followed me and accepted me as your leader, in time you will accept her as one of us. This is what I wish. We will begin preparations this day and tonight, under cover of darkness, we will commence our journey.'

Fierce saw no need to mention that she also had been threatened. She must remain tight and in control, the invincible leader of a very small but proud Gypsy band. The group broke up muttering amongst themselves. Some shrugged, ready to accept the decision of their leader. Others shook their heads and began to argue with each other. It remained to be seen just how loyal they would be by nightfall when their journey would commence.

Fierce strode over to where Chloe and Pippin were preparing to start their daily chores before leaving for the market. 'I have decided to leave this field and travel north.' She watched the colour drain from Chloe's face. 'But do not fear. You will be coming with us for your protection, and also for mine, I fear. We must leave and leave quickly before we are hunted down like pigs.'

'But the police…' Chloe began.

'Do you really think they can protect you when these witch hunters have only one thing on their minds? They are craftier than you might imagine. Our only hope is to flee for safer country. Pippin, on the other hand, is not in danger. He has some stable work and Harry is far too old to travel.'

Pippin could not argue with that. 'But Miss Chloe here is my friend. I do not want to lose her,' he protested.

'If she stays, you will lose her forever. She will be hunted down and burned as a witch or, at the very least, tortured and thrown into the river to drown. Is that what you want for her?' Fierce challenged him.

'No. I don't want that. If you say that this is the only way, then I have no choice but to accept, do I?'

'No, I'm afraid you do not. And Chloe, you must see that this is the only way. You will be safe with us. Without us, your future is dangerous indeed.'

'I understand, Fierce. I'm not happy leaving Pippin behind, but I know he'll be all right and I know that he has a future ahead of him. I would not wish him to be placed in jeopardy because of me.' Chloe sighed and looked fondly towards Pippin. 'I trust you, Fierce, more than I think I have ever trusted anyone in my entire life. I think.' she added with a small smile.

'Good. Then we must prepare to be ready to leave this night. Agreed?'

'Agreed.' Chloe moved closer to Harry to give him a pat. 'You'll look after Pippin, old Harry, won't you? And you, Pippin, walk with confidence and hope into your future. You had better be going or the smithy will think you have deserted him.' She gave him a quick impulsive hug and waved him off.

22

Dick's mind, bathed with Henry's excellent ruby port, pondered lazily on recent events. Chloe's image floated in front of him, followed by the brief yet clear image of that other woman so much like her at Mrs Montgomery's benefit. It didn't make any sense at all but then his present life was more than a bit of a mystery.

Chloe was definitely not a witch, thanks to his twentieth-century intelligence, but he was afraid for her in this untrusting climate where folk were still acting on their superstitions. She was in danger and Dick couldn't explain to himself, let alone anyone else, why he should feel such a responsibility. Was it because they were both outsiders and that was where his sympathy lay? He knew nothing about her. If she had a twin sister, then surely she would know. He wanted to ask her more questions, hoping it would in some way shed some light as to why he was here. The Gypsy camp leader was a little intimidating but not enough to stop Dick looking for answers. Sleep finally overcame him and he slipped into the arms of Morpheus without resistance.

Sounds of a commotion interrupted Dick's dreams and he woke with a start. The noise was coming from the kitchen and he immediately went to investigate.

Nellie was arguing with a young girl who seemed distressed. 'Now then, dearie, no need to get all het up. I'm sure it's only a misunderstanding. Now, let's have a look at her arm here.' Nellie was examining the arm as Dick walked in. 'There is a bruise and another one lower down. Why did he hit you?'

''e was accusing me of stealing and I never,' cried the girl. 'I've been cleaning his cottage for over a year now and all of a sudden he takes to me with his heavy hand. 'e says I'm a witch! and I'm not, I'm not!' She continued her sobbing.

At this point Dick intervened. 'Hey, what's this all about? Who accused you of being a witch?'

The girl shrank behind the generous body of Nellie.

'She was getting some provisions at the market when two men approached her, grabbed her arms and began the accusations. Very frightening, I'm sure,' Nellie nodded.

Dick looked from one to the other. The habit of witch calling was becoming more widespread. The young girl was plainly terrified. She had no obvious recourse for protection and was a sitting duck for the abuses of these ignorant trouble makers.

'What's your name?' Dick asked her gently.

'Florrie,' she replied in a whisper.

'Well, Florrie, you come with me. We'll go to the police and you can make a statement. They'll look for these offenders and bring them to justice.' Dick didn't quite believe his own words, but it was a start.

'Me?' she replied. 'But I can't write, and who would listen to me? I'm only a cleaning girl.'

'Don't you worry about that. I have a friend who will listen. Will you come now?'

'Dick m'boy, quite frankly, I'm a little worried.' Henry looked at Dick over his glasses as they sat in the now familiar tavern. 'That poor girl is scared out of her wits and who will look out for her? Have we no idea who these thugs might be?'

'Well, it could be the same ones who attacked Chloe last week. All brawn and no brains with no thought for consequences. Apart from that, I have no clue.'

'We can put out another alert in the hope that someone will come forward, but folks get scared with this sort of thing and are afraid of repercussions. We can't give a bodyguard to every person who is attacked or who might be in danger of being attacked, do you see my dilemma?'

'Yes, Henry, I do. We must hope that someone will be brave enough to come forward so the police can apprehend the perpetrator. It's a slim chance but it's all we've got at the moment. My concern is that they will grow in numbers, spreading fear and untruths among poor and more ignorant souls. But you are right, of course. Er, dare I ask how is Chloe?'

'Last time I saw her, she was fine but she couldn't help with information either. She's still wary but I plan to visit her again this afternoon, just to check.' Dick smiled grimly. 'You know, I'm afraid that this is all coming to a head since she arrived in these parts, wouldn't you agree?'

'Reluctantly. Reluctantly, I must say. Are folk that worried about strangers? Now that concerns me greatly. There is a growing, prevailing belief in witches, strange as it may seem in our modern society, but we must face it.'

Dick suppressed a smile at the reference to society. 'Yes, I suppose so. Anyway, I shall see what I can find out this afternoon.

Dick was beginning to enjoy his sorties on horseback. It was, indeed, just like riding a bicycle and as he trotted along the lane he entertained the thought of finding a nice little plot of land with a cottage and perhaps a horse of his own. Locked in his reverie, he arrived at the Gypsy camp.

He pulled up sharply at the gate and with a shock saw that the field was empty. No wagons, no Gypsies, no fires, no horses grazing – completely empty. Now he was more than worried. Of course Chloe would have gone with them. He looked up the lane but saw nothing; no sign of a small Gypsy travelling band. His mind raced. How on earth in this time and place could he track anyone down? He urged his pony to a trot and, looking carefully at the tracks made by wagon wheels and horses' hooves, followed in the same direction.

An hour passed, maybe more, when Dick fancied he could hear the sound of small bells, such as those on a horse harness. He coaxed his mare to a canter, peering into the distance. He would have to make haste before nightfall or he would be in danger himself. The Gypsy band would not be going at a fast pace, he guessed, so by now he should be gaining on them.

He reined in his pony, stopping to listen again. This time he could hear singing. He continued at a slower pace, not wanting to frighten the travellers with his sudden arrival.

His mare began to behave in a peculiar way. She began stepping from side to side, snorting softly and bobbing her head up and down. What was she sensing? There was something she knew that Dick didn't. He remained calm, waited for her to settle before continuing, but she didn't settle. She began to neigh, keening and low as if she was mourning a fellow creature. Now, the hackles on Dick's neck were beginning to rise. He could sense some sort of danger himself now, but saw nothing and heard nothing.

Now she was stamping on the ground, trying to rear up, stamping more, and all the time neighing as if trying to communicate with her own kind.

Then without any warning, a sharp wind whipped up out of nowhere, gusting up the lane, swirling leaves and twigs around and around, then up and over the hedges on each side. The sharpness of the wind lashed Dick's face, tore at his hair, threatened to snatch the reins from his hands. His mount was now rearing up, screaming in fear, pawing at the air, coming down with a heavy thud, then rearing up again. Dick felt the roaring of the wind in his ears and the stinging of its force on his cheeks before he was thrown up in the air, landing heavily on the rutted track.

When he came to, Dick's mount was nowhere in sight. Debris was all around him, tree branches that had been ripped from their trunks, trees themselves uprooted and lying across the path. Not two feet away, were the bodies of some birds as if they had been hurled out of their nests and dashed onto the ground. The air was eerily still; no sounds of bird or beast, no rustling of bush or tree; no sign of life at all.

The stillness was like a death. Dick struggled to his feet, noticing that his clothes were torn to shreds. His face hurt, his head ached, his body felt bruised and battered as if he had been in a battle and lost the fight.

He staggered to the hedge and looked over into a field. He was shocked by what he saw. There were five or six cows lying still and lifeless on the ground. A huge tree nearby had become uprooted and fallen with all its aged might on these poor animals. Still there was no sound on the air. A catastrophe had happened. Were Chloe and her band of Gypsies safe? Or had they been wiped out by this phenomenon of nature, for surely that is what it was. Dick's common sense told him it was just a storm but he couldn't help wondering what other forces had been involved. Was it just a storm?

23

'Good lord! Dear boy, what on earth has happened to you? Come in, come in!' Henry opened wide the door and Dick all but fell in.

'I don't know, I…' and before he could utter another word, he collapsed into Henry's arms.

Later, having been given some warming, nourishing soup made by Nellie's capable hands, Dick felt restored and could relate his experiences to Henry.

'But that's impossible! There has been no change of weather – not here anyway. It has been a calm spring day with sunshine and just a light zephyr breeze. I don't understand. It's not as if you have been to the other side of the world.' Henry laughed at his little joke. 'You look as if you have been through hell. What happened to your mount?'

Dick shuddered. 'At first I thought she had run off but she hadn't. When I came to, I heard the most pitiful moaning, and when I had gathered some strength, I walked to where the sound was coming from. And there she was – the mare, lying on her side further up the lane. Her head was twisted, she had a terrible gash in her flank and, as I moved nearer, she looked up at me with a dreadful terror in her eyes, shuddered and then she was gone. It was awful but she was in so much pain. How could anyone do something so cruel to an animal? And what will I tell the smithy?'

'You can think about that later. You have been traumatised and must rest a while before you do anything. And Chloe? Did you find her?'

'No,' Dick moaned. 'She has gone. The whole camp has gone. The field is empty and I followed the tracks for some way until this, this thing whatever it was, whipped up and attacked! I tell you, Henry, it was the weirdest thing. Most unnatural.'

Dick woke feeling very out of sorts and quite groggy. He heard voices in the adjoining room, then the door opened slowly and John and Henry tiptoed in.

'Henry has just told me. How extraordinary. Of course we must organise a search party and try to find your friends! Surely they can't be too far away.' John smiled encouragingly.

'Well, after what that storm did to me and everything else around, I wouldn't be sure that they're still alive. It was vicious. I've never seen nature behave like this before. But I must find out if Chloe's all right. We must go as soon as possible.' He looked up anxiously at the brothers Fielding.

'Yes, well, it will take a day to organise some searchers. I just can't summon them up like magic,' Henry said.

'Well, no longer,' replied Dick. 'I have bad feelings and I'm very, very worried.'

When he was alone again, Dick tried to get his thoughts together. He felt very tired but that mustn't get in the way of the search. He would manage because he had to. He dozed lightly for the next hour or two then, feeling somewhat refreshed, he washed and put on some clean clothes.

The stallholders were beginning to put their wares back in boxes and very few people were wandering through now as the day drew to a close. Dick noticed that Lily was still there.

'Lily! I'm glad you're here. I'm worried about Chloe. She has left with the Gypsies and I don't know where they've gone. There was a terrible storm last night…'

'No storm here, sir. Quiet as a baby sleeping, it's been. All day,' Lily interrupted, anxious to get on her way. 'I'm sure Miss Chloe knows how to look after 'erself.'

'She didn't come and say goodbye to you?'

'Well, she did in a sort of way.' Lily said pensively.

'What do you mean?'

'She came to see me and just said that she wouldn't be by for a few days as she was feeling a bit poorly. Now, if that was a goodbye, well, I never knowed it at the time. I said I hoped she'd feel better and that was that. Now, if you'll excuse me…' Lily began packing up.

Dick hurried to Oliver, the smithy. He was also finishing for the day, the embers of his fire dying down.

'Oh, dear. Oh, dear,' Oliver repeated as Dick explained as gently as possible what had happened to his mare. 'But I don't understand. This storm you keep talking about. No storm here. Are you sure you haven't been dreaming? She was such a lovely mare…' Tears began to form in his tired eyes.

'No, there was truly a most terrible storm. I have never seen anything like. Most unnatural, and no one has been able to explain it. I certainly can't. I was nearly killed myself. And Chloe has gone. The Gypsies left that morning. Pippin will miss her.'

'Yes, he is missing her already but he's a good lad and works industriously. He will be all right.' Oliver sat down on an upturned log and put his head in his hands. 'Something's not right, is it?' He looked up at Dick.

'No it isn't, but I'll be going out with a search party to see if Chloe and the Gypsy folk are safe. I'm so sorry about your horse.' Dick placed a comforting hand on the smithy's shoulder.

'Not your fault, lad,' said Oliver softly. 'At least I know now what happened to her. You couldn't have seen the future, let alone prevent it bringing about a tragedy. I hope you have some luck with your search.'

'Thank you. I bid you goodnight.' Dick managed a smile, grateful for Oliver's graciousness.

As he walked away from the market grounds, he sensed he was being followed. He turned his head quickly to see two figures slip behind one of the tents. He walked on more quickly, then ducked behind a large bush. Holding his breath, he peeked to see if they were coming his way. They were but went past and Dick recognised them as two of the burly drinkers he had seen at the tavern. He began following them at a safe distance, holding his breath whenever they stopped. He managed to stay out of sight but not out of the sight of another one who was right behind him and, before he could run, he felt a jaw-locking punch and a thumping to his kidneys. As he was slipping into unconsciousness, he heard his attacker swear.

'Serve ye right, you witch lover. We don't want your sort in these here parts. This is a warnin'.'

Henry and John were not amused when they saw the state of Dick some hours later.

'You are foolish to set off on your own. We can be strong as a team and you must promise you won't try to do it again. Do you want to jeopardise any chance we have at tracking down your friends and apprehending these ruthless assailants?'

Dick didn't miss the anger in Henry's voice and apologised. 'I just thought I could…'

'Well, you did not think it through. Now, get some sleep because I am hoping that by noon tomorrow we will have an adequate number of searchers to come with us.'

Dick was compliant and, feeling like a chastised schoolboy, went to his box room.

24

Two days of travelling and Fierce and her little band of Gypsies were tired. She had noticed a field not a mile back and took Flare to see if she could find the owner.

'We can stay here,' she shouted happily as she came trotting back with the good news.

And soon, small fires were set and lit and the smell of roasted meat wafted through the early night air.

Chloe and Fierce sat on the steps of the wagon, sipping tea.

'We are being lucky with the weather,' said Chloe. 'It's such a superb evening but I miss Pippin and Harry, you know. I do hope they're all right.'

'They will be perfectly fine. And we will be fine too. We will continue tomorrow morning at first light, so we must have an early night. I am going to sleep out here but you must sleep in the wagon, Chloe.'

Chloe knew better than to argue with her protector. Although exhausted, she couldn't sleep. She watched the stars in the clear sky through the little wagon window. She thought about Pippin, Harry and, strangely, the man who had come to see her at the other camp. She would never know now who he was or why she appeared familiar to him, nor why he seemed familiar to her.

The smell of coffee tickled Chloe's nose and she opened her eyes to bright sunlight. Dressing hurriedly, she stepped down to bid Fierce good morning. A cup of coffee was balanced on a stone beside the little fire and Fierce was close by attaching the harness to Flare in readiness for the continuation of their journey.

'Did you sleep well?' she called out to Fierce.

'Like a baby. And you?'

'Eventually. But I'm rested and ready to go. How far do you plan to travel before you think we'll be safe?'

'I will know. I will know when safer ground has been reached. You mustn't worry about that. We will have a good day's travel and, with God on our side, we will find yet another field where we can shelter. Are you ready to go?'

Chloe nodded and, within the hour, the little Gypsy band was back on the road.

One of the Gypsies, a man with a short beard and dark, flashing eyes, started up a tune on his fiddle. His body swayed in time with the music and soon the other travellers joined him in song. Chloe listened entranced, wishing she could sing along, but she was an outsider and could only listen to the haunting traditional music with wonder and a touch of envy.

Fierce, however, wasn't singing. She appeared to be deep in thought and was somewhere else. At first she didn't respond to Chloe's nudging.

'Fierce. Fierce! Why aren't you singing? I know you have a beautiful voice. I've heard it before. Please sing. For me.'

'I'm not in a singing mood, I'm afraid. I am thinking ahead about where we will be this night. I felt all was going relatively smoothly and that we have left any evil behind. But now I'm not so sure. There is an ill wind blowing and it is blowing towards us. We must change the course of our journey.'

She cried out to the others. 'Halt! We must make a different plan.'

The riders, wagons and horses stopped as if as one.

Fierce jumped down from her wagon and marched around to the front of them. 'We will turn at the next fork to the left. You will have to trust me to lead you all to safety for if we go on ahead as we were, danger lurks ready to overtake us. Quickly now. We must arrive at a suitable destination and it must be before nightfall.'

With many murmurings, the little band regrouped and pared off at the next left fork on the road.

'You're not really worried, are you, Fierce? So far, all has been quiet and no one has followed,' Chloe said.

'Ah, Chloe dear, you are still not learned in the ways of our people. I am sensing danger and we must avoid it if possible. I am your chief custodian now and because the two of us have been accused of being witches, we must be very, very careful. Please trust me on this. And even so, I cannot completely guarantee our safety. I will do my best and that is all. Do you understand?'

Chloe nodded and reached for Fierce's hand. 'Well, let's be off, then. And can we have some more music? It lifts everyone's spirits and certainly lifts mine. And will you sing this time, please?'

Fierce laughed softly. 'All right, then. I will sing if it makes you happy.'

25

Dick swung himself up into the carriage which he was sharing with Henry and John. Others followed in assorted conveyances. Some were on horseback and led the way. They were behind the little Gypsy band by about two days and therefore had a lot of ground to cover. With a jerk, Henry's carriage lurched forward and Dick felt his heart lurch as well. He asked himself why all this mattered so much and why he should care so much about what happened to Chloe.

They passed the field where the Gypsies had been. They passed the place further up the track where the freak storm had thrown Dick off his mount and where the dead cows still lay in the field waiting for the crows to finish them off. Dick shuddered at the recent memory. Then, to add to his concern, a brisk breeze appeared out of nowhere, unsettling the horses, blowing the trees into a frenzy. Then the wind stopped as quickly as it had arrived.

The horses whinnied then quietened under the mastery of their handlers. Nerves had been jangled a little. No one spoke and the party continued their journey, eyes on the alert, every muscle tensed for whatever might lie ahead. Yet nothing further occurred. No bandits. Nothing out of the ordinary. They might have been going on a picnic, so tranquil did everything seem. The sun warmed them, the birds sang to them and everyone began to relax and chat amongst themselves.

'Well, I don't know about you, Henry, but I still feel a bit weird. You know, that calm before the storm feeling that you get sometimes when you just know that something is going to happen?'

'Mm, yes, I have had that feeling a few times in my life. But,' Henry chuckled, 'not for the longest time, I am happy to say.'

'Well, I won't be able to relax until we catch up with Chloe and company.'

'I'm sure we are concerned for nothing. It is not unusual, you know, for Gypsies to move on. That's what they do for reasons best known to them. Chloe obviously wanted a bit of a holiday and seemed to have forged a friendship with their leader, what's her name again?'

'Fierce,' Dick replied.

'A strange name, don't you think? Anyway, I'm sure we will find them safe and sound. Dick, can you take the reins for a bit? I feel like a bit of a nap. Thanks, dear boy.'

Dick had had minimal experience with carriage horses but as they were only walking, he thought he might be able to manage. How hard could it be?

They travelled along in this fashion for several more miles. Until, there was a shout up ahead.

Dick reined in his horses, coming to a rather abrupt halt. Henry nearly fell off his seat, waking up suddenly.

One of the horsemen up front had trotted down to Dick's carriage. 'Come and have a look at this.'

Dick hopped down and went to see. He almost expected to see a clue, a piece of clothing, a headscarf or something that would let them know that they were on the right track. But instead, it was another witch poster nailed to a large tree at a fork in the road. He caught his breath. This was not a good omen. This meant that the assailants who had attacked him had come this far and were spreading their venom. But he also noticed that there were wheel tracks turning off to the left.

'They've gone this way,' he shouted, sounding much more confident than he felt. 'The tracks look fresh.' He hoped he was right.

Dick looked grim as he raced back to the carriage and climbed in. 'I fear we may be too late. We must hurry now and not travel at a snail's pace any more. Please, Henry, take the reins. I'm not as able as you, and you know how to quicken the pace of your steeds.'

Their carriage rocked from side to side as Henry urged his pair to a quicker pace. He used the whip sparingly but the horses responded as if they had been waiting for permission to have their heads.

When Henry finally reined them in, they had been travelling at some speed for nearly an hour. Their flanks were frothy with sweat, their mouths over salivating.

'We must rest them a bit,' said Henry as they slowed down to a walk. 'We'll stop here in this glade. Dick, can you reach for that costrel* back there, please. They will want a drink.'

'This contains water?' asked Dick surprised. 'How quaint.'

'Quaint it may be, old it may be as well, but it is useful and doesn't take up much room. You'll be surprised as to how much water it does contain.' Henry smiled. 'But I've got two! Whoa, boys. Stand now.'

Henry gently sponged down his pair and poured water into an old wooden bucket he had untied from the side of the wagon for them to drink. He was perspiring profusely as the day had warmed up considerably.

'Time for us to have a rest too.' He took the lead and sat down under a leafy oak.

About three hours of daylight remained by the time the search party resumed their journey. Dick was silent, lost in his own thoughts, the motion of the carriage soothing him. Henry whistled under his breath and John, who had been dozing a good deal of the way, began to sing softly.

*The costrel, a leather flask, was produced from before the seventeenth century through to the early eighteenth century and could have been still in use up to at least the mid-eighteenth century if looked after.

26

Chloe felt relaxed now, more than she had been all day. Listening to Fierce singing was like being a child again, with the soft crooning of a mother's voice lulling her infant to sleep. She felt her eyes closing, but not for long. Without warning, Flare reared up, whinnying loudly. Fierce tried to rein him in but he was spooked by something. He thudded back to the ground, pawing it frantically. Then, before Fierce could restrain him, he took off as if all the demons in hell were chasing him.

The wagon rocked violently, as it had no choice but to follow the frightened animal. Chloe bumped up and down, gripping the rail in front of her, her knuckles white with fear as she swayed from side to side. Fierce yelled out to Flare but he took no notice, overtaking the other Gypsy wagons. The other horses were not spooked at all and the Gypsies looked around in surprise as their leader went around them and sped up ahead, totally unable to control her mare.

On and on Flare galloped, the adrenalin building up and giving him extra impetus as the wagon wobbled in his wake, nearly becoming airborne, rattling as if it might be torn asunder at any minute.

'Fierce!' cried out Chloe. 'Make him stop! We'll be killed if you don't stop him!' She screamed as she nearly lost her seat and would have been thrown by the side of the track had not Fierce reached out and steadied her with one hand, quickly returning it to the taut reins as she tried desperately to rein in her terrified Flare. 'I'm doing…my… best! He's so strong. I don't understand what frightened him.'

Fierce was breathing hard now and her words were almost lost in the noise of rumbling wheels, the thudding of hooves, and now Chloe screaming in absolute terror, her face pale, her body rigid as she clung to the railing.

'Hang on for dear life, Chloe! He has the devil in him and there's nothing I can do. He'll stop when he's ready, and only then. I'll try and drive him into the side hedges, but I doubt if I'm strong enough.' She yelled. 'Hold tight! I'll try.'

She planted her feet as hard as she could to the footboard, pulling the reins to the right towards a large hedge just coming into sight. Sweat was beading on her forehead, her lips drawn in a tight line as she strained and strained to rein Flare in to do her bidding.

'I can't! I can't, Chloe. He won't respond! He won't listen! I'm trying as hard as I can!' Fierce cried out. She was giving her all but it wasn't enough and Flare galloped on and on. All she could do was to let him have his head.

'If you pray at all, Chloe, do it now, for I fear we are lost if he doesn't stop soon. The track is narrowing. The wagon can't take any more of this.' As she cried out, there was a loud splintering crack and the wagon shuddered. 'It's going to break up, Chloe. We'll have to jump off or we'll be killed! Try and steady yourself and when I say go, jump! We have to do it. It's our only hope.'

'I can't!' screamed Chloe, holding on even more tightly to the swaying van. 'I can't jump! I can't jump. I'll be killed!'

'You'll die if you stay. Now, get as close to the edge as you can and when I count to three, jump. Please, Chloe, do it for me!'

'All right!' She sobbed now but moved as close as she could to the edge of the footboard.

'One, two, three!' Fierce gave her a little nudge, letting go of the reins for a brief instant.

Chloe leaped, landed first on her feet but the shock threw her body onto the grassy verge and she rolled back towards the track, just missing the back wheel of the wagon as it careered past her. She managed to sit up in time to see Fierce standing up, still trying to rein in Flare. At a bend in the track, the wagon swerved, toppled, righted itself then it was gone and Fierce with it.

'Fierce!' Chloe yelled. 'Fierce, wait! Fierce!' but the Gypsy leader was out of sight now and Chloe collapsed to her knees, crying out hoarsely, tears coursing down her dusty cheeks. 'Oh, Fierce!' She struggled to her feet, staggered a little then, regaining some equilibrium, began to run after the wagon.

27

A sudden jolt of the carriage woke Dick from his blissful reverie. 'John! Look! Up ahead, there's someone lying on the road! Stop!'

'Mercy me,' exclaimed John as he pulled his pair up. 'Mercy me, I do believe it is a woman! Dick, there's a good lad, hop down now and take a look.'

Dick was already down and raced towards the inert body lying in the middle of the dusty track. He touched her shoulder but there was no response. He turned her slowly to face him and gasped in shock. It was Chloe! He lifted her wrist and felt for a pulse. It was very faint, but it was there, slow and tentative. She was unconscious and Dick carefully lifted her in his arms and carried her to the carriage.

'My word,' said Henry, who had woken with the sudden jolting stop of the horses. 'It's Chloe! Where are the others?'

'Where indeed?' muttered Dick as he and John managed to heave her into the carriage. 'I think she's all right, but I'm not a doctor. What do you think, Henry?'

Henry also felt for her pulse, listened to her breathing and gently felt for signs of broken bones. 'The pulse is there but it is weak. Still, she is breathing quite evenly and I can't detect anything that is broken. She may have hit her head. Look,' he pointed, 'there is a rather nasty bruise on her forehead. Wrap this knee rug around her and we'll keep travelling in the same direction. There's no point turning back having come this far. Dick, you support her head and keep her still. John, give her a small sip from your brandy flask.' Henry had taken charge.

'Brandy flask? How did you know I had one?' John asked.

'Oh, for goodness sake, John! You always carry it with you and thank God you do. Now hurry, man. The poor woman is cold and needs some warmth in her vitals.'

Dick lifted Chloe's head very gently so John could dribble a little of the brandy into her mouth. Almost immediately, she began to cough as the burning liquid went down into her throat. She opened her eyes and tried to sit up.

'No, Chloe. Just take it gently. You've had a nasty fall, I'm guessing. Slowly now. Let the brandy do its job.' Dick gave her an anxious look.

'Oh, my head. It does hurt!' she moaned. 'And Fierce! She was going to jump with me and she didn't. She lost control of Flare and now she's gone. Who knows what might have happened! We've got to follow and find her.' Chloe began to sob.

'Now, now, Chloe,' started Henry, being rather fatherly. 'Don't you start worrying yourself. You have had an unpleasant experience. Just give yourself a little while to recover your equilibrium. We'll catch her up, don't you worry. She can't be too far ahead.'

'But you have no idea just how fast the wagon was going! It was starting to splinter just before I jumped off! She might be dead by now or in the hands of the witch hunters. We mustn't waste any time. Please! Hurry!' She sat up. Some colour had returned to her cheeks.

Henry saw the earnest expression on her face. 'All right. All right then, we'll give the horses the hurry up.' Henry clicked his tongue, sent a message through the reins and the carriage began to gather speed.

28

Fierce felt the blisters stinging her hands as she pulled on the reins. She could only hope that Chloe had survived the jump from the wagon but now was not the time to worry about that. Sooner or later, Flare must get tired and, no sooner had she thought that and as if he had read her mind, he began to slow down, his nostrils flaring, foam spurting from his mouth.

'Whoa, boy. Whoa! That's it, boy, good boy. Slow down now.'

Flare slowed finally to a halting stop. Fierce jumped from the wagon to calm him down, stroking his sweaty flank, his neck, murmuring soft words in his ears. He would not be travelling any more this day, so she unharnessed him. She unhooked the pannikin hanging at the back of the wagon and filled it with water from her bottle. He stopped panting, drank his fill and moved to some grassy clumps on the verge.

Fierce was exhausted. Her hands smarted from the raw blisters and she tore a strip from her underskirt, wrapping it round them. This wasn't a safe place to stay for the night, but she had no choice. She had not seen any other wayfarers the whole time she had been on this godforsaken road and hoped there would not be any now.

After tethering Flare, she climbed wearily into the wagon. Anything loose had been tossed around as if a high wind had been inside. She collapsed onto her bunk. Thoughts of Chloe weighed heavily on her mind and she wondered if the rest of the Gypsy band were still on the road worrying as to what might have happened to their leader. But fatigue won and within minutes she was fast asleep.

Dick and his party had been travelling for some hours. A darkening sky threatened to sent down torrents of spring rain and Henry decided they should look for a more comfortable place to spend the night. There must be a field somewhere with an old barn they could use for shelter.

Suddenly, 'Look!' said John, who had been casting an eye out for anything unusual. 'Over yonder in a field. There is a small fire.'

'Yes! I can see it,' cried Dick. 'In fact, there's more than one fire. I suggest we investigate.'

Henry tethered the horses and he and Dick found a farm gate. They opened it cautiously and approached the fires.

'Excuse me, good people,' called out Henry. 'Would I and my friends be able to share your hospitality this night? We have no shelter and we have with us a young girl who is most unwell and needs rest and warmth.'

A burly, bearded man stood up and walked towards him. He was not altogether unfriendly but not very welcoming either. 'Who would you be, then?' he asked.

'My name is Henry Fielding. This is Dick, and my brother and the young girl, Chloe, are waiting in the wagon.'

'Did you say Chloe?' rapped out the man.

'Yes, do you know her?'

'She be the friend of our leader, Miss Fierce. Only God knows where she may be now. The demons took her horse and wagon and disappeared.' He stared in the direction of the carriage. 'What be the matter with her?'

'She had to jump from Fierce's wagon because it had started to break up and the horse wouldn't or couldn't stop. She hurt her head and is in some shock.' Henry hoped the man would be compassionate.

'Jumped? Well, it wasn't our fault, was it? We would have come across them, only,' he paused, shifting his feet about, 'only, we took another track so afeared were we of them demons we heard tell of. Well, I suppose you can stop the night then. Best bring in your carriage. Who knows what travels abroad in these here parts. We must continue our journey as soon as dawn breaks, mind. Our leader will need us. Wherever she may be,' he muttered, beckoning to Henry.

Henry waved to John to bring the carriage into the field.

The small band sat around their fire and did not get up when the strangers entered. Their faces were ruddy from the heat of the flames and one or two had pots cooking something on the coals. The odd whinny from a horse pierced the night air and, as John moved the carriage forward, one of the men jumped up and gestured to a place away from the fires and under the lee of a number of tall green trees. Once he had tethered the horses, he joined the others, and the burly man who had greeted Dick motioned for them to come and sit with the other members of the Gypsy band.

Dick chose to remain with Chloe, who was lying down on the carriage seat. She was very pale and cold to the touch. Dick took off his long coat and draped it over her. She looked so childlike and vulnerable. Her breath was coming in short gasps and he wondered if she had a broken rib or had damaged her back. Every now and then, she would cry out in pain, but her eyes didn't open and she remained semi-comatose.

Dick had never felt so helpless. Back in his own time, an ambulance would have been summoned. But in a world without electronic communication, fate had to be welcomed because that's all there was. If Fierce had been here, at least something could have been done to help relieve Chloe's pain. But Fierce herself could be in dire circumstances. She might even be dead. It was impossible to surmise.

Just then, Chloe stirred. Her eyes flickered as if they would open at any moment. As her chest rose and fell with each painful breath, Dick was horribly afraid. Her eyes flickered again, opened ever so briefly, made contact with his eyes then closed slowly, as one last breath left her body and she was still.

Dick felt a sob rise in his throat. He hardly knew this girl and yet…yet there had been some unexplained connection. Now, he would never know. He kissed her gently on the forehead, placed her hands across her body and covered her completely. She would feel no more pain. She would no longer be tormented by those who wished to harm her. She was at peace and Dick would be the harbinger of bad news when he caught up with Fierce.

'Dick, dear boy. What is the matter?' Henry knew as soon as he had uttered the question.

'She's gone, Henry. Just like that. The fall must have done more damage than we thought. And I couldn't help her!' Dick said angrily. 'What do you do for a doctor in this god-damned century? If she had been able to go to a hospital, perhaps she would have survived. Even if I had my mobile phone with me, it probably would not have worked way out here in the middle of nowhere. No communication towers, not even an old-fashioned phone box. I wish I'd never come here. It's worse than the middle ages.'

Henry said nothing but followed Dick back to the carriage and confirmed what Dick had told him. 'Poor girl,' he said softly. He placed a hand on her head.

'She didn't deserve this.' Dick felt a lump in his throat. 'We will catch them, Henry, won't we? The thugs!'

'Now, dear boy, don't upset yourself any more. We will track them down, don't you worry. You did all you could. Miss Chloe was badly injured…'

'She damn well was and there was nobody to help her!' Dick interrupted angrily.

'Unfortunate. Most unfortunate. But people do die. We all die, you know. It's just a shame that one so young and beautiful should die so soon. But we can't control fate, dear boy.' Henry patted Dick's shoulder. 'We must take life, and death, how we find it, I'm afraid. And we must lose no haste in taking care of Chloe's, er, remains. I shall ask the Gypsies if we may hold a ceremony and perhaps bury her here.'

'You can't do that!' Dick was horrified. 'You don't know who owns this field. We can't just dig a hole and dump a strange body in it and tick off. We'll be arrested.' The irony of his comment was not evident at first. He was challenging a law maker.

'Do you have a better suggestion?' asked Henry quietly.

Dick's brain was feeling scrambled. This was a situation he could never have ever imagined being part of. Oh, he knew he could have handled it in 1997, but here?

'No,' replied Dick. 'I'm out of my depth here, Henry. I'm sorry. You know what's best in your time. I will follow your lead.'

'Thank you, Dick. We must be expedient. Come with me and we will talk to the burly one. He seems to be in charge.'

The burly one, whose name was Alfred as it turned out, was more amenable than Dick had thought. 'I had a sister once,' he said. 'She was about Miss Chloe's size too and sweet as the new season's apples she was. We was travelling at the time, on the way to a market, as I recall. She got sick, see, and had a high fever. She didn't last more 'an two nights. Terrible, it was. We had to stop and bury her in a place we didn't know. Terrible, it was. Terrible. Just like it is now for poor Miss Chloe. There are some in the camp who didn't want Miss Chloe around, but it wasn't their decision, was it? Our leader Miss Fierce chose her and I respected that. And I will help you with the burial. I have a large shovel in the van and, after it is done, we will have a small ceremony, as long as you don't mind that it is a Gypsy one. Of course, it will be a little different as Miss Chloe wasn't a Gypsy.'

'We understand,' nodded Dick. 'Thank you for being helpful.'

The earth was soft and pliable and a neat grave was soon dug. Chloe's body was wrapped in a colourful cloth. As there were no intimate personal possessions, Dick drew from his little finger a small ring he had worn since his university days and placed it in one of the folds of the cloth. It was a ring of some significance – his first love, in fact – and it seemed fitting that a young girl like Chloe should take it with her.

Alfred lit some candles around the body where it now lay beside the grave. 'We must keep vigil this night and bury her tomorrow at sunrise,' he announced.

The Fielding brothers and Dick exchanged glances. They did not want to waste more time but it was necessary to give Chloe a respectful funeral and they prepared themselves for a long night.

The women in the camp managed to find some flowers, which they formed into a wreath and placed it at Chloe's head. As everyone settled by the light of the campfires, the Gypsies began to chant in Romany. It was strangely soothing and Dick sat with his head bowed, random thoughts racing through his mind. If he ever was able to return to 1997, no one would believe what he had experienced. No one.

Dawn came quietly, gently as one by one the watchers stirred, stretched their limbs and shivered.

The candles had gone out and the grey morning light cast a sombre shadow over the small corpse lying beside its final resting place. The Gypsies began to chant softly again, coming forward, and with much grace and decorum slowly bent to lift Chloe and lower her into the ground.

Dick stood beside the grave, trying to remember some Christian words, mumbling them to himself. One of the women handed him a single flower, indicating for him to throw it into the grave. He nodded his appreciation and watched the fragile flower float down to settle on Chloe's body. He then helped the others to fill in the grave and it was over.

'I can't explain the loss I'm feeling,' Dick said to Henry afterwards. 'I barely knew her and yet there was something…'

'Life can be puzzling. Perhaps she reminded you of someone you once knew. Someone back in the, er, in your time?' John offered as he stretched his stiff joints.

'Maybe,' acknowledged Dick. 'I guess I'll never know, will I?'

'I think we should prepare to depart once we have thanked our hosts. We must make up for lost time.' Henry, as usual, led the way.

29

Fierce stirred. A soft breeze was caressing her cheek. She sat up, peering through the little window. To her relief, Flare was still there, grazing as if nothing had happened. Fierce knew something had happened. The mystery was ever deepening but somehow a truth or two would be revealed. Just when was hard to tell.

Fierce looked around the damaged wagon. She got up and began to tidy up the mess as best she could. As she stepped outside afterwards to inspect the wagon for damage, she was shocked to see how bad it was. A large split ran along the length of one side. One of the wheels was damaged perhaps beyond repair. A few windowpanes had been shattered but that was nothing. The wagon might just roll again. She decided to wait a day to see if her little Gypsy band would catch up. She couldn't fix the wheel by herself. She didn't have the right tools, but she repaired what she could.

Flare seemed all right but, on further inspection, there was a sizeable gash in his left flank. She hoped her herbal antiseptic would help and reached for the box. To her horror, it had been forcibly dislodged and it was in pieces on the floor, most of the vials shattered and empty. Flare would just have to rely on nature to heal his wound. She would be forced to stay here for more than a day and only hoped nature would be kind to them.

But she couldn't remain here on the side of the road. She walked on a little further and discovered an old broken-down gate half off its hinges. The opening was to a small field. No animals grazed, the grass was long and there appeared to be no sign of life. Could she take a risk, harness Flare to the battered wagon and make it to the field? She decided to try.

With much creaking and lurching, the broken wagon submitted

148

to Flare's valiant pulling and very slowly and painfully crept towards the field up yonder. Fierce was afraid it would break up some more, or that the wheel would finally disintegrate completely, but the grace of God intervened and the wagon limped into the field. She felt relieved and safer now and looked forward to seeing her band, who would most certainly have picked up Chloe. Was she all right? She might have broken an ankle after jumping from the wagon.

She couldn't understand why her wagon had been singled out and taken on a terrifying ride almost to the death. What had spooked Flare? Questions, questions and more questions flashed in and out of her tired brain. Her body shivered and she felt suddenly cold despite the arrival of the sun.

Yesterday, the road had been empty and she saw no sign of the witch haters, save for the odd poster, but that was way back, just before Flare was frightened. She didn't want to believe in evil forces as she wasn't superstitious but what other explanation was there? That strange wind: just a freak of nature or something else?

The following morning, as Fierce was stirring, she heard the familiar sound of trotting hooves. With heart pounding, she gingerly stepped down from the wagon and crept over towards the road. To her amazement, a rather genteel carriage was approaching with three men. One of them looked familiar and as she peered more closely she saw that it was the man who had visited Chloe and had been at the market a few times.

'Whoa,' cried Henry as his pair drew to a halt opposite the gate.

'Hello there. Miss Fierce?' Henry, always polite, called out.

'Of course it's her,' interrupted Dick testily. 'Oh, Fierce, it is so good to see that you're unharmed. But I'm afraid that Miss Chloe was badly injured. We found her on the side of the road and tried to save her, but it was too late. She…she's with the angels now.' Dick wondered why he said that. He supposed it might have been to soften the blow he had just delivered. He also remembered that many Gypsies were of the Catholic tradition.

Fierce stood rigidly beside the gate. The colour had drained from her face and she put out a hand to steady herself on the railing. 'It was my fault. It was my fault. I told her to jump. My fault! I thought it was the only way she could be saved from a certain death but I condemned her to it by my actions. Oh, poor Chloe. Did she suffer much?' Fierce couldn't hold back her tears.

'She was mostly unconscious. I stayed with her until the end,' said Dick. 'We caught up with your Gypsy band and they were wonderful. She had a Gypsy burial. We couldn't bring her with us. We had to leave her there. She's now at peace.'

'I can't believe it,' Fierce said softly. 'Did you know that I had made her my Gypsy sister?'

'No, I didn't know that,' said Dick.

'Well, you had better come through. I am planning to wait for the others to catch up. I need help to repair my wagon. It is a miracle I am alive but why take Chloe? She never hurt anyone and she was so frightened of those who were persecuting her.' She pushed back the old gate a little further. 'Come. You will tell me more.'

Fierce made some tea. The little fire looked so lonely but she hadn't yet been able to gather much wood.

'I'm sorry you have been through so much,' Henry faltered. 'We will get them, you know, sooner or later, and they will pay for their actions. Miss Chloe paid a terrible price because of some folk's superstition and ignorance. I would not like to see that happen again. And you, Miss Fierce, will need to be very vigilant. I am thinking that it might be a good idea to stay here for a while. To lure the beast, if you get my meaning. You will be well protected. Travelling the roads will make us more vulnerable, whereas here we can stand strong. There will be enough of us, I am sure, to withstand any assault.'

'An assault? Is that what you think could happen? Sir, you don't know what these fellows are capable of!' Fierce interjected. 'They are ruthless. They have one thing on their mind and that is to hunt down anyone they think might be a witch. In this case, probably me. Do not think for a minute that you will be able to reason with them. It might be 1779 but witch hunts still happen and there will be no mercy shown if they catch up with me. You could all be in danger for supporting me! Do you know what they do to a witch? Do you? There is a man called a witch finder. Oh yes, still. The suspected witch has to undergo a scratching process. If she doesn't bleed, it is deemed she is a witch. Women have had their hands chopped off, vicious iron helmets forced onto their heads with a sharp steel prong that pierces the tongue. They have had screws inserted into them and, as if that torture is not enough, they are either thrown into the river to drown or they are burned at a stake. Do you still want to stay now?'

'Of course we do,' spoke up John, usually the taciturn one. 'You were Chloe's friend and we know you are not a witch – why, that's plainly ridiculous! We can't have a damsel in distress, now can we?' he chuckled.

'Hear, hear,' chorused Henry and Dick.

'I'm sure that by tonight, your Gypsy friends will be coming by. We'll take turn at keeping watch, not just for them, but for anyone who is not welcome here,' said Henry.

'What about you, Dick?' asked Fierce quietly.

'Well, it goes without saying, doesn't it? You've been kind to Chloe and now it's our turn to look out for you. Sooner or later, our witch hunting thugs will reveal themselves. And then justice will be done. You'll see.'

Fierce wasn't convinced but she said nothing this time. She was a very independent woman but was secretly glad now of a bit of male support, or any support for that matter. She sipped her tea thoughtfully, watching the three men chat amongst themselves. Her eyes wandered to where Flare was tethered. He seemed content and if his flank was hurting, he didn't let on. Nature was perhaps doing her job.

Fierce turned her attention to Dick. He was a strange one. Not at all like the brothers. He seemed as if from another world and that was what he and Chloe seemed to have in common, she suddenly registered.

His speech, although now a little habituated to the prevailing one, was foreign-sounding. He knew things that she had never heard of. He spoke of places she never knew existed. Yet he seemed to be a kind man, albeit rather emotional when something stirred him. And those clothes he was wearing! They didn't suit him one bit. Why, he would look more relaxed if he was attired in the Gypsy style.

Dick was suddenly aware that Fierce was scrutinising him and turned to return her gaze. She looked down and focused on her tea

'If anyone is hungry, I can find something for us to eat. There's not much in the wagon, but I expect when the others get here, they will have some more. I shall go and check to see what is in the larder.' With a little forced laugh, she left the men by the fire.

30

Fierce watched Henry tend to his pair. John was sitting beneath a huge oak tree deep in thought. He wasn't a talkative one but he looked very tired. Playing policeman didn't suit him. Henry, on the other hand, was intensely interested in everyone he met. In his quieter moments, he would appear very pensive, often writing something down in a small black book he carried with him.

Fierce was curious about people who wrote. She had never learned to write anything but the basics. Always busy with household chores when she was growing up, it wasn't deemed necessary for the young girls to learn to read and write, although her mother used to teach her a little in secret so now she could at least read simple things. Like the rude warnings that had been left nailed to her wagon door. She shuddered at the thought of them.

As she lay on her bunk later that night, she could hear the murmurings of the three men as they chatted on around the fire. Every now and then, soft laughter would drift in through her little window. She felt a little envious of their camaraderie and felt the tears start again as she thought of Chloe, the sister she had wanted but was now denied. She reminded herself that she was tough. She was the leader of a Gypsy band and would stay strong for them. Her own feelings must stay in the background. To be weak was to be vulnerable and that was dangerous, especially now when she needed all her strength. Eventually she slept, but fitfully, dreams punctuating her rest.

Fierce awoke to the clamour of voices. They're here! Thank God, she thought and went out to greet her Gypsy friends. Once again she heard the story of Chloe's death and thanked them for their care.

'I have decided that we must rest here for a time. And in that time, perhaps those vicious thugs who wish to do harm will be lured here like the fly to the spider's web. You have met Dick, Henry and John of course. They have offered to add to our numbers and I for one am glad they will remain. What say you?'

For a moment, there was silence. The little band were aware of the fragility of their leader for the first time and although they would have preferred to move on, out of loyalty to her they agreed, one by one, to stay.

'Thank you.' Fierce lifted her head and smiled. 'Now, let's get some repair work done. As you can see, my wagon is in very bad shape. With your combined skills, I know you will be able to restore its usefulness. If a few of you could do some hunting, for we are bereft of food, tonight we will eat together to celebrate our reunion and to mourn one of our own: my sister, Chloe.' She turned and strode back to her wagon.

'Do you think the city will be missing us?' Henry mused as he settled himself against the trunk of a sturdy tree.

'Probably, but we can't let them know what is happening, now can we?' John, always the practical one replied.

'Oh, I know, but I was just wondering. I mean, it is as if we have all just vanished off the face of the earth. Nellie will be concerned, for one. She will wonder why we have not come home for supper. But I suppose it cannot be helped. I miss my port wine,' he added ruefully.'

'I have to say that I do too, Henry,' Dick laughed. 'I'm now just a wayfarer with no abode, no wherewithal, no prospects and charged with the onerous task of apprehending some criminals who so far are elusive. I don't look forward to meeting them either, even though I know we must, sooner or later.'

'A matter of time, dear boy. A matter of time. Patience is a virtue and I am sure that ours will be rewarded all in the fullness of time. Will you look at the stars in the sky! Magnificent. Such beauty above and yet it doesn't touch some of the ugliness down here, does it?' Henry sighed, looking up at the celestial entertainment. 'May our task be not too onerous when it presents itself.' With that, he drew his cape about him and closed his eyes.

Dick did not feel sleepy. He wandered about the camp, occasionally looking up at the stars himself. A comforting reminder that at least in the heavens, all was well. He passed Fierce's wagon and therein a candle still burned. He thought of knocking on her door but it seemed inappropriate after the taxing time she had been having.

Fierce was aware someone was passing. She blew out her candle and peeked through her little window to see Dick walking away in the direction of the horses. He looked out of place in a Gypsy setting. Who was he, really? With many questions vying for attention in her head, Fierce lay down, eventually closed her eyes and slept.

<h1 style="text-align:center">31</h1>

Dick woke, cold and shivery. There were no embers left in the fire. He yawned, turned his head in the direction of Fierce's wagon. He noticed something stuck on the outside of the door but couldn't see what it was. Curious, he wandered quietly over and saw the crude piece of paper with its message:

> One departed, now ye know,
> she who lives is soon to go

There was no movement within the wagon. She must still be asleep. Should he tell her about the message? His instinct was to protect her, but he was her guest. He ripped it off the door and as soon as she emerged, he would show her and be there to offer words of comfort if needed.

But he was disturbed. How could anyone slip in to the camp, unnoticed? Someone must have been awake to see, surely. An awful thought hit him. What if one of the Gypsies was the culprit? That was just too terrible to contemplate, so he put it out of his mind. She was good to her people and they liked her and were loyal. After all, they agreed to stay here in support.

Dick would keep watch himself this next night. He would warn Henry and John and ask them to do a watch as well.

Fierce reacted strongly to the note. 'How dare they come into my camp? In the stealth of the night like that. I will keep watch tonight and if it happens again, they will be very sorry.'

Inside, she was quaking. That the note deliverer had come so close. Why, he could have entered the wagon itself! Perhaps next time…but she would make sure there was no next time. Bit by bit the thugs were coming into the trap. She didn't quite know just what the trap was, but if everyone was on the alert, they would be caught. Eventually. What did Henry say? In the fullness of time? Well, she had time. She had time for revenge because of Chloe's death. She had time for revenge because her mother was put to death as a witch. Oh, she had the time. Her blood was boiling. A strength she thought was lost began to rear up inside her.

'We will get them, Fierce. Don't you worry about that!' Dick tried to sound positive and certain. 'Now, tonight, I shall keep watch right outside your wagon and I don't want any opposition from you. No arguments!' He waited for her to explode.

'You will freeze to death. It is cold at night. And look at what you are wearing. No, you can wait inside with me. Neither of us will sleep, but that can not helped.' Fierce had made the rules. Again.

'Um, won't that be misconstrued? I mean, with me being in here. With you. In your wagon?'

'Don't be ridiculous. This is a plan. Have you got good ears?'

'Good ears? As good as any, I suppose. I do have excellent eyesight.' Dick smiled.

'Good. It is settled. We shall warn all the others to be on the lookout.'

Dick didn't tell her that he had already arranged for John and Henry to take watch. 'Good idea,' he agreed. 'What time shall I come over?'

'At night time of course.'

'Right. Night time. When it's dark?'

'Of course when it is dark! What is the matter with you?'

Dick smiled. As long as Fierce stayed mad, she would stay strong. Night time it is, he whispered to himself.

32

Henry sat bolt upright. He had been leaning against a tree on his watch. He must have dozed off and he was cross with himself. He heard the noise, but it was only the noise of the horses shuffling around, wasn't it? He stood up, stared into the darkness. Was that a shadow moving past the horses now? The shadow moved now, into the open.

Dick, who had been sitting leaning against the little wagon window, saw the shadow too. It moved forward in the direction of Fierce's wagon. Now he saw two shadows!

Henry had seen two also. He nudged John, woke him up, and the two men began following the two shadows as discreetly as possible.

Dick now saw four shadows, not knowing that two of them were Henry and John. He motioned to Fierce to be still, then opened the door of the wagon quietly and noiselessly. He stepped down and moved around to the side, flattening himself against the wooden hull. He held a heavy fire poker, clenching it until his knuckles must be turning white. He waited until the two shadows were almost at the door then struck. At the same time, Henry raised an arm and with his weapon, brought it down heavily. Two figures crumpled to the ground.

Fierce lit a candle and came outside. The light was weak but it was strong enough to make out the features of the two intruders. Henry recognised one as being the talkative man from the tavern. Dick recognised the other one. It was Oliver, the smithy.

Once the alarm had been raised, men came running from all directions, some with rope to tie the intruders up. Oliver was carrying a piece of paper, no doubt to be plastered upon the door of the wagon.

'Oliver! How could you! I thought you were a trustworthy man. Pippin works for you! Do you realise what you're doing? Do you care that an innocent girl might be accused of something that she isn't guilty of?'

Oliver looked down. 'They said that Chloe girl was a witch. I was promised some money for helping to apprehend her. Business has been slow. I didn't mean no harm.'

'Rubbish! You did mean harm. Do you know what they do to women they say are witches? Well, let me tell you.'

Dick leaned into Oliver's face and recounted everything he knew about the cruel methods used for witch punishment. Oliver's face changed colour several times.

'And,' continued Dick, 'it's all because of ignorance, stupidity, greed, fear, because there's no such thing as a witch. Get that into your thick skull. Well, now you'll have the full force of the law brought against you. This man,' he pointed to John, 'is a magistrate and he'll deal with you once we get you back to London Town. And your friend, that low life you came here with,' Dick paused for breath. 'Take them to the carriage and make sure you tie them very, very securely. We'll return to town first thing tomorrow morning.'

Two of the Gypsy band came forward and led the criminals away.

Fierce touched Dick on the shoulder. 'Thank you,' she murmured. 'I really did not believe we – that is, you, would catch them at it. I can not believe one was Oliver. I always thought him to be a nice man. Well, you just never can tell. I guess you have to get to know people really well, don't you, Dick?' She gave him a half smile, turned and went back into the wagon.

Dick thought of following, but the stake-out was over. There was no need to be in the wagon with Fierce now.

The next morning, the Gypsies began to pack up.

'We'll be moving south,' said Fierce. She had walked over to the carriage where the two criminals were securely settled under the watchful eyes of John and Henry. 'Dick, what will you be doing back in London Town?'

'I'll be helping John streamline the police force where I can. After that, who knows? I doubt I'll find a job as a lawyer anywhere.'

'Is that what you did back where you come from?'

'Yes, but being here has made me reflect on my past life. Perhaps there's something else I'd like. Writing has always appealed so maybe I'll write my life story.' He laughed.

'I do not think you have lived enough life yet,' quipped Fierce. 'But whatever and wherever you decide to do it, I hope it pleases you. I doubt we will meet again and it is a pity it was under such grave circumstances. I am thankful for your help and I will remember you always.' Fierce put out her hand.

Dick grasped it firmly. 'I think I'm going to miss you, Fierce. Stay well and keep out of trouble.' He winked.

'And I you, Dick. Think of me now and again, and Godspeed.' She drew in closer to him, kissed him lightly and pulled away. She walked quickly back to her wagon, turning just once to wave, her gold earrings glinting in the morning sunlight.

'Penny for your thoughts, Dick, m'boy.' Henry turned to his friend.

'Oh, I was just thinking about everything that's happened lately. An adventure in a way, but I've found some nice friends and I've learned a lot from you and John, from poor little Chloe and also from Fierce.'

'It sounds as if you are going to leave us. Are you?"

'Well, not for a while. Where would I go? I'm still very much a stranger in these parts. There would be no regular work to match the qualifications I have. Do you know, Henry, I might just take a few days in the country. I've loved it around here and perhaps I might do a little exploring somewhere else. Would you mind? Just for a few days.'

'I think that would be capital, m'boy. You have earned it. Would you like to borrow a carriage? I have a horse that would love some outings – she has not been out for a while – and I have a spare carriage, not as grand as this one, mind you, but it would more than adequate for your needs, I am sure. Mellie would pack you some food and drink and you could ride off into the sunset and have a little holiday. How does that sound?'

'Oh, Henry. It sounds too good to be true. Are you sure you want to lend me your carriage? I seem to have developed a habit for trouble.'

'Nonsense. Circumstances. That is all it was. Circumstances. Happen to anybody. Now, hop aboard and it is off to London Town to deposit these two n'er-do-wells in a not too comfortable gaol.'

33

The steady clip-clop of hooves on cobblestones was almost musical. Once Dick had cleared the town limits and was on a narrow country road, the sound changed. He could have been imagining it but he could swear that the little mare pulling Henry's second-best carriage was enjoying herself immensely.

They were both escaping in a way, off to a country adventure. The mare needed very little encouragement. She seemed to know just where she was going and Dick was quite happy to let her have her head. Just the steady trotting sound was soothing to the soul and he didn't much care how long it took. Sooner or later, they would come across a little inn where he could bed for the night without worrying about criminals and witch hunters.

He reflected on the life that Fierce would be leading and hoped she would be safe now. He traced the features of her face in his mind and committed the image to memory. He would miss her feisty, stubborn ways and he smiled to himself as he remembered.

34

Good lord! Was that the time? He would be late for court.

Dick jumped out of bed, noticing that his wife had not even slept there last night. He was puzzled but not worried. He had ceased to worry about some of her strange behaviour since she had joined the, well, cult. He could think of no other word for it.

The kitchen was cold and he flicked the switch of the air con. The jug boiled quickly and as it switched itself off, the phone rang. The office, probably, to remind him he was late.

'Mr Fortescue? Mr Richard Fortescue?'

'Yes,' replied Dick tentatively.

'County police here. I'm afraid I have some rather bad news for you. It's your wife, you see. She was involved in a nasty car accident last night. We couldn't contact you. She was taken to St Ann's hospital but passed away very early this morning. I'm so sorry. We did try to reach you, but was your mobile switched off, sir, perhaps?'

'Yes, er, no. I don't remember. Oh, my God.' Dick began to tremble. 'I haven't been myself lately. My wife is often late home after meetings she attends. Attended. Oh dear. Can I go to the hospital to see her?'

'Of course, sir. I am very sorry.'

'Yes, thank you.' Dick replaced the phone in its cradle on the wall, barely unable to stop his hand shaking. He felt himself pale. His skin was clammy and he was slightly dizzy. Chloe dead? He could not believe it. They had been going through some very difficult times with their relationship and Dick often wanted to just disappear, but dead? Chloe?

He rang the office quickly. He explained quickly. He left the house quickly and drove, also quickly, to the hospital. Why the hurry, he couldn't tell. Perhaps he was in a hurry to confirm the news. Perhaps he didn't quite believe the police officer. It was all a big joke.

As he hurried through the door leading to the emergency ward, he nearly knocked a woman flying as she was coming out.

'Sorry,' he muttered, looking at her face briefly. A strangely familiar face, but he was in a hurry.

The woman looked back at him, brushing her long, dark hair to one side, a gold earring glinting in the early morning light. 'That's all right,' she said, smiling briefly. 'I wasn't looking where I was going either.'

www.ingramcontent.com/pod-product-compliance
Lightning Source LLC
Chambersburg PA
CBHW030205130726
47898CB00012B/884